DEAD BEYOND THE FENCE

A NOVEL OF THE ZOMBIE APOCALYPSE

BRIAN KAUFMAN

DARK
SILO
PRESS

Dark Silo Press
P.O. Box 1712
Fort Collins, Colorado
80522-1712

Dead Beyond the Fence:
A Novel of the Zombie Apocalypse
and
Dread Appetites
A Dark Silo Press Book / March 2010
Copyright 2010 / Dark Silo Press / All rights reserved

ISBN # 978-0-615-34578-9

Cover Illustration: Jack Larson
Back Photo: Tiger Kaufman
Cover Design and Text Layout: Michael St. Clair

First Printing: March 2010

Printed by
Lightning Source

For my children,
who may eventually forgive me.

The red sun crawled over the lip of the world like a severed head. Angel sat in the stuffed chair near the window with her arms wrapped around her legs and a blanket draped over her shoulders. Resting her chin on her knees, she watched the birth of another day. The sun's rays shot through the blinds, locking her against the chair with bars of light. She was quiet. The studio apartment was small, and Kevin might wake up.

She'd been in the chair for nearly two hours. Some mornings, she stayed under the covers, awake, rigid with sorrow, her eyes clamped shut. Other mornings, like this one, she left him in the bed. Kevin was young, and things were simpler for him. They'd made love the night before and now he was sleeping. He was in love with her. He had no idea what she was thinking.

No matter. Once the sun was up and the day was underway, she would be fine. She would cope.

A knock at the door woke Kevin in an instant. He pitched forward, blanket spinning off the bed, the gun in his hand. He stood next to the wall, blinking, a strand of hair dangling in front of his eyes. Half awake, he looked down at the Ruger. Then he looked at Angel. He gave her a rueful smile, shrugged and lowered the gun.

The knock came again. He went to the door and stared through the peephole. "It's Torgeson." She pulled the blanket up under her chin while Kevin undid the door chain.

Rick Torgeson was the president of the Resident's Association, a soft, puffy man with thinning blond hair. Though he whispered at the door, Angel could tell Torgeson was upset. His thin, wet lips twisted out some request, his fingers knotted together in front of him as he spoke.

Kevin stood with his back to her. His shoulders slumped, only a little, but enough. Angel's stomach, already a fist, clenched tighter.

Kevin nodded and closed the apartment door. He came back smiling, but he spoke in halting sentences, as if thinking furiously while he dressed. "It's probably nothing. They just want my help. Insurance, I guess." He put the handgun at the foot of the bed, and slipped into jeans and a tee shirt.

"Rick seemed upset."

"We're behind on rent," Kevin said. He glanced up, hoping for a laugh or a smile. She stared.

"There's trouble on the fifth floor," he admitted. "Do you know what I did with my socks?"

Angel sat up in the chair and looked out the window, down this time. They were on the third floor. "What's happening?" she asked.

"Nothing, I hope." He slipped his bare feet into his shoes and picked up the gun, putting it in his lap. He looked into her eyes. "Remember what we talked about the other day?" She didn't answer. "About leaving?"

Her eyes widened and she began to pull at her hair, blond ringlets that she tugged straight and then released. "I remember."

"It'd be a good idea if you put some things together. Fill both backpacks. Jam them full. Mine already has some of the important things in it. The compass. The fire sticks. I don't think this is the time, but we've done pretty well for ourselves by being cautious." He paused. "It's probably nothing. I'll help you unpack when I get back."

When I get back. The words chilled her. "How long will you be gone?"

"If I'm gone more than an hour, send the search dogs," he joked.

She turned again to the window. The sun was eye level now, glaring at her. She glanced down at the apartment lawn, but there was no comfort there.

"Lock the door behind me," Kevin said, standing up.

"Do you want the flashlight?"

"No. Pack it."

Angel struggled to her feet and followed him to the door. She crept across the faded green carpet, each step taxing her to the point of exhaustion. Kevin walked slowly, pausing every few steps to let her catch up, talking all the while. "Make sure you pack the maps and the binoculars. And pack that blue nightgown of yours. What did you call it? A teddy? Pack that. It's too valuable to leave behind, hahaha."

"Be careful," she whispered. She wanted to say more. She wanted to say how grateful she was for his patience and for his protection. But there was no energy, just piercing sunlight and the black tar of despair.

"I'll be back," he promised, touching her cheek with his fingertips before slipping into the hall. Angel stood wavering, her gaze fixed on the closed door.

The door popped back open.

Kevin stuck his head through. "I said lock up!" His idiot grin caught her off guard, and she found an unlikely smile. He winked. "See you in a little while."

And then he was gone.

Kevin met the others in the stairwell. The elevators had been out of commission since the power company shut down. The building had its own generators, two gas-powered units grinding away in a small room on the roof, but fuel was limited, and with winter coming, the residents had elected to restrict power usage, authorizing only the hall lights, the outdoor floods and the video cameras.

"Okay, what's the plan?" Kevin asked. There were five others, all armed. One of the men had a pump shotgun. Todd Baylor from the fourth floor carried an Uzi knock-off. Rick Torgeson and the others carried handguns.

"We're going up the stairwell together," Torgeson explained, his voice ripe with false cheer. "We go in the door together. We stay together. We find out what the situation is, and we solve it." He wiped his mouth with the back of his hand.

"How many others are coming?" Kevin asked.

"This is it," Baylor snarled. He was ex-military, in his late forties. "Everyone else decided to sleep in. Remember that when you need help." His teeth flashed through his silvered mustache as he spoke.

Kevin turned to Torgeson. "If there's a problem, five people won't fix it."

Torgeson waved him off and opened the door to the stairwell. "Don't worry. There can't be more than one or two of them. The stairway is locked on the inside. No key, no entry."

A door opened behind them. Louis Mason stepped into the hall carrying a gun and backpack. "You joining us?" Kevin called out. Mason shook his head no.

Torgeson started into the stairwell. Kevin pushed past the others, catching Torgeson at the first step. "How bad is it?" Kevin asked.

"I don't know."

"Bullshit. How bad is it?"

"It's not that bad."

"Mason is leaving. How many people are leaving?"

Torgeson tried to wave him off.

4

"Are you losing your nerve, son?" Baylor asked, fingering his mustache.

Kevin ignored Baylor. "How bad?"

"You know how these things happen!" Torgeson cried, spraying flecks of spit into Kevin's face. "Someone takes their own life, and no one disposes of the body. But I know something else—we have defenses here! We have power and we have supplies!"

Kevin's gaze narrowed. "We have defenses, but this keeps happening."

Torgeson gave a helpless shrug and started up the stairs. Baylor followed him. The others waited. Kevin didn't recognize any of them. He tried to smile. "Okay, guys. Let's go fix things." He didn't look back as he climbed the steps, but he could hear the others follow.

Torgeson stood at the fifth floor entrance, his face pressed close to the thin, rectangular window in the door. "The hall lights are out," he said. "They're the only lights we allow, and they let the damned bulbs go out."

Kevin glanced at Baylor. The older man scowled and looked away.

"I brought a flashlight," offered one of the men behind Kevin, passing it up to Torgeson.

"Well! There's nothing stopping us then. We should go in." Torgeson slipped the key into the lock with some difficulty. His hands shook. "I'll go first, I suppose."

No one spoke.

"I'll go first," he repeated. He turned the key, and pulled the door open.

The hallway was dark. The stale smell was no different than on the third floor, a good sign. Torgeson stood in the doorway, flashlight on.

No sign of movement. After a long pause, Torgeson cocked his pistol and stepped into the hall, holding the flashlight and the weapon in front of him. He pointed the light from side-to-side, turning his torso with the flashlight's thin beam. "All clear," he said, his voice wet with panic.

From just beyond the door on the left side, a shape stepped into the open doorway, arms reaching. With a single step, the shape embraced Torgeson, who screamed and dropped his flashlight.

Without thinking, Kevin moved into the doorway, put his gun against the attacker's head and pulled the trigger. The Ruger bucked in his hand and the man's head exploded, crumpling at the point of impact. The back of the skullcap erupted into chunks of tissue and bone fragments that tumbled down the black hallway. The man's body jerked once and dropped to the carpet.

Torgeson stifled a sob. He knelt to retrieve the flashlight, patting the carpet furiously, unable to take his eyes off the corpse. At last his hand closed around the flashlight barrel. He stood, clutching the light to his chest like rosary beads, whispering a prayer of thanks.

"You have your balls back, I see," Baylor said to Kevin. Baylor stepped over the corpse, which lay on its back, chest heaving.

Kevin scowled. He stepped past Torgeson, tearing the flashlight from his hands. He played the beam into the corners of the stairway alcove, making certain there would be no more surprises. The others stood back in the stairwell, afraid to come through the door.

"Come on, boys," Baylor called. "We still have work to do."

Torgeson waved the others in, but his attempt at cheer dissolved into helpless, frightened giggling. The man with the shotgun poked his head through the doorway. "What are we supposed to do now?" he whispered.

"Room-to-room," Baylor said. "It's the only way." He glanced at Torgeson. "That all right with you, boss?" he asked, grinning through his mustache.

Kevin disliked Baylor. The man seemed to enjoy what had happened to the world, as if liberated by tragedy. It grated on Kevin to need him. But the truth was, Baylor was worth considerably more to him than a good-hearted incompetent like Rick Torgeson.

The dark hall looked like a death trap. Smoke and stench from Kevin's gunshot filled the shadows. And some of the other residents were already leaving.

"We have to stick together," Torgeson said. "Together, we can do anything. Alone, we're nothing. . ." His voice faded away.

"I need your keys," Baylor said. "Carson, you watch the rear." The man with the shotgun nodded. "The rest of you, get up here. Brown? First door on the left is yours."

Kevin nodded. He wouldn't have to work point in every apartment. He preferred to get his turn over with. He gave Torgeson the flashlight and checked his pistol. While Baylor put the key in the door, Kevin glanced back. Was someone creeping up on them? He couldn't tell. A small, dim rectangle of light hung in the darkness behind them—the window in the stairwell door. There wasn't enough light to see anything else.

Kevin turned back as Baylor opened the first apartment. The smell hit immediately. There was no mistaking the wet vegetable smell or the foul stench of ruptured intestine. The door jerked open from the inside, and a man stumbled his way forward, clawing at them. A thin film covered his vacant, expressionless eyes. Dried blood smeared his lips. Kevin raised the gun and fired, missing. Hands reached for him, inches away. Kevin stepped back, firing again, striking the man in the temple, staggering him. He fired a third time, finding the forehead this time, spraying the entryway with a brown mist. The man dropped to the floor, blocking the door.

Kevin leaned back against the doorframe. "Sorry. I usually shoot better than that."

Baylor touched Kevin's shoulder with the barrel of his weapon. "Reload before you go in."

"Of course." He stepped back out of the doorway and fished bullets from his jeans pocket, reloading with trembling fingers.

"I think something's moving down the hall," Torgeson moaned. He pointed the beam, but there was nothing. "Never mind."

"Damn," Kevin said. Torgeson was losing it. He would be no help, and there were more apartments to search. Kevin took a deep breath and stepped back through the doorway.

It was too early for the sun to warm the apartment rooms, but sweat rolled into his eyes anyway, blinding him. His gun hand shook.

The curtains gaped open, lighting the room. The entryway led to a living room. To the left was the kitchen. Kevin pivoted in place, trying to avoid a sudden attack. The kitchen was empty. To the right, a hallway led to the bedrooms.

Kevin steeled himself. This wasn't going to be easy. Each floor had eight apartments. And there were ten floors in all. Would they have to secure each and every room? And would they all be like this?

He paused before the first bedroom, planning his move. He would step into the open door, turning left, gun pointed. If someone moved, he would have a split second to decide whether or not to fire. A footstep behind him sent a shock along his spine. He turned; ready to shoot.

It was Baylor. "Just watching your back, son," he said. Baylor pointed in the direction of the first bedroom. "Smells like hell in here, doesn't it?" Kevin let out a breath and turned back. He gave himself a three-count, and stepped in front of the door.

He had only an instant to take it all in—the canopy bed, pink bedspread, open window, closed closet door and the doll. The dresser had one drawer open. Kevin blinked. A shadow flickered on the far side of the bed.

A soft thump.

He slipped into the room and sidestepped to the right, gun in front. A tangle of hair bobbed just past the mattress. He took another two steps and stopped.

Angel began packing the moment Kevin left the apartment. Kevin had plenty of gear, including the .32-caliber pistol. He said it had stopping power a .22 didn't. She'd fired the pistol once. It made her wrist sore, but she could hit a stationary target.

They had several boxes of granola bars left, the crisp kind that didn't go stale quickly. She filled the canteens with spring water from the grocery store. As she worked, the crippling depression faded, replaced by an increasing sense of urgency. There was a limited amount of space in the backpacks, and so much to take—the maps, the water filter and the box of ammo for Kevin's .44, now only half full.

The teddy. He'd said to take it. She shook her head, wondering whether to laugh or cry. She put it in the pack.

There was a chance he wouldn't come back. What if he didn't return? She would be lost. He should have told Torgeson to fuck off. The man was forever knocking at the door, pressing them for one favor or another. Kevin was always on the front line. He was always in danger.

Where would they go if they had to leave the apartment? The first floor was walled up and supposedly unbreachable. The video cameras were added insurance. What could have gone wrong?

It was Kevin who'd suggested an escape plan. The Dexter family on the second floor had suffered an incident just two weeks earlier, and though it was contained, it was clear that any problem could escalate out of control without notice.

She glanced at her watch. Kevin had been gone for an hour. The vice that crushed her temples cinched tighter still. If he didn't come back soon, she would go looking for him. And if the worst happened, she would end the suspense, and be thankful for the release.

<hr />

Kevin walked from the apartment, pale and shaken. He leaned against the wall, spitting. The little girl's smell was in his nose and mouth. The sound of automatic weapon fire came from inside. A few moments later, Baylor stepped to the doorway. He nodded sadly at Kevin.

Kevin scowled, wiping his lips. The sound of screaming came from down the hall, or perhaps from above. It was impossible to tell.

"Can we move on to the next apartment?" Torgeson asked.

"I'm done," Kevin said.

Baylor tensed. The others looked too frightened to speak.

Torgeson took a deep breath. "We have to go on, Kevin."

"You said one or two at most. There have been three so far, and we're one apartment deep. And that's just this floor. How many floors have a problem?"

"Just this one! I swear it!"

"So far."

"The video cameras!" Torgeson protested.

"Haven't helped. This place crawls."

"You can't just quit!" Torgeson wailed. He trembled, tears welling in his eyes.

"I'm leaving," Kevin said. He hoped Angel had their equipment packed.

Baylor stepped closer. "I didn't take you for a coward."

"I didn't take you for a fool," Kevin replied. The two men eyed each other for a moment.

"I'm not leaving," Baylor said. "This is my home. I'll not give it up."

Kevin closed his eyes. "If I stay here, I can't take care of Angel."

Baylor snorted. "Where will you go? Where's the safe place?" Kevin was silent. "Who will watch your back if you leave? And who will watch mine?" His argument made, Baylor squared his shoulders and marched down the hall to the next apartment.

"He's right! You can't do this!" Torgeson began to plead, but his words couldn't dispel the memory of the little girl thrashing on the floor by the side of the bed, a hole the size of a half-dollar torn in her cheek, her pink tongue poking through the opening as if trying to taste the air. The man at the apartment door, the one Kevin had killed, had blood on his lips. Was it the girl's blood? She'd been no more than six or seven years old. She should have been playing with her doll, or riding a bicycle. She should never have been on the floor, her broken legs splayed out, shards of bone jutting from under her kneecaps. If she could have walked, she'd have come after Kevin. He would have had to shoot her. Instead, Baylor did it for him.

The apartment building was no longer defensible. It was time to leave. As he walked away, he heard Torgeson talking to the others.

"We don't need him. One apartment, and he's given up! Selfish is what it is. Selfish! This is a community! We have to look out for one another!"

Kevin took the stairwell down, gun ready to fire. He was accustomed to being afraid. It was a season of fear. But the sense of panic he felt was new. The clock was ticking. He could feel it.

Two floors later, he put his key into the stairwell lock. There were sounds from below—a thump, a closing door. He didn't stop to wonder.

Angel's heart stopped when she heard the key in the door. It had to be him. *Please let him be all right.* Then he stepped into the room, and she was angry with him. She wanted to berate him for going away, for being dramatic, but she was in his arms instead, kissing him, touching his face. He looked like hell.

Kevin held her. He smelled her hair, pressing her slender body close. Then he let her go. "We have to leave."

"How bad is it?"

"Bad, and getting worse by the second. Are we packed?"

"Yes."

"Did you get the maps?"

"Yes."

"All of the food?"

"Yes."

"And the teddy?"

She put a finger to his lips. "We're packed."

He sighed. "Okay." He put on his jacket, grabbed his pack from the bed and strapped it on. The small plastic ammunition box sat at the foot of the bed. He checked the box, frowned and jammed it into his front pocket.

Angel slipped her jacket and pack on as well. She tucked her blond curls into her canvas hat. The tee shirt she wore went halfway down the thighs of her jeans. She patted the shirt in place and looked up.

"You look cute," he said.

"You're an idiot."

Kevin took a last look around the room. "Okay, let's go."

Kevin opened the door first and peered into the hall. Angel waited, fighting the thought that hounded her mornings; *I want this to be over. Life is too hard, too much of a struggle. And it will end in blood and teeth.*

When he turned back, Kevin's expression had changed. He locked eyes with her, a half-smile on his lips. "I want you to know how important you are to me," he said. "You were a good boss, and now you're the most important thing in the world to me."

"Oh, God."

"Keep close, but not too close, in case I need to back up. Don't look around a lot. Keep your eyes on the middle of my back. And be ready to run."

She could feel what little energy she had draining out of her. "Are we finished?"

He took the gun from her hand. "I love you," he said.

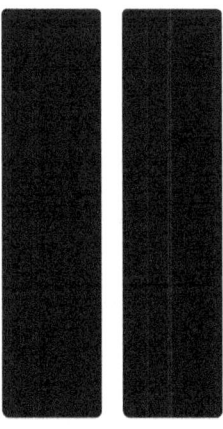

They crept to the stairwell. Screams echoed from the floors above. Kevin descended the stairs, Angel's fingertips at his back. With each turn, he stepped out, gun in front. When they reached the ground floor, he checked the chain and padlock on the door to the outside.

The stairwell had been bright and open once. Now plywood and tabletops covered the glass, braced from behind with discarded furniture. Kevin put a finger to his lips and crept down the last set of stairs to the basement. Angel followed reluctantly.

The basement door was locked. Kevin reached into his pocket for his keys, fumbling past the ammo box. "This is why I made them give everyone a maintenance room key," he muttered.

Angel stared back at the stairwell, startled by the slam of a door from several floors above. "The door is padlocked," she said. "How are they getting in?"

"They were already in," Kevin said. He pulled the keys free and unlocked the deadbolt. Gun extended, he pulled the door open.

Pitch black.

"Well, that's not good," he said. "Which backpack has the flashlight?"

"I don't remember," she answered, near tears. Footsteps sounded in the stairwell, followed by another slammed door.

"You've got to open them up and look. I'm going to keep this gun pointed. Okay?"

"I'm sorry." Her voice crumbled.

He stood still, the gun aimed into the dark. "Just find it, okay? Once we get through here, it's sunlight all the way."

She removed her pack and opened the top, glancing behind her every few seconds. If something came down that stairwell, she would break. She knew it. She dug her hands into the pack, fishing for the light.

"Any luck?"

"Not yet," she whispered. "I think it's in your pack."

He shrugged his left shoulder, sliding out of the strap, his right hand still pointing the Ruger. He switched gun hands carefully and slid out of the remaining strap. Angel took the pack and set it on the ground.

"No hurry," he said. She couldn't tell if he was being ironic. She unbuckled the pack and shoved her hand in, thrashing through the supplies she'd carefully packed. "I can't find it. Oh God, did I forget it?"

Another door opened above, followed by a woman's scream—this one closer to the basement. The piercing sound jolted her, and the pack slid sideways, falling over on the concrete floor. She tried to pick it up, but her hands shook and she couldn't grasp the pack's frame. She felt a hand on her shoulder and looked up. Kevin stood, his gun still extended in the direction of the door, a calm smile on his face. "It's okay," he said. His voice was a deep, warm blanket. He glanced at the doorway, and then looked back at her again. "It's in there. You wouldn't forget. Take your time."

"God-God-GOD!" someone screamed.

Her hand brushed the barrel of the flashlight. She jerked it free and handed it to him. He turned back to the door and pointed the beam inside. "Tie up the pack and help me get it back on," he said, his voice wavering.

Looking up the stairs was slowing her down, but she couldn't stop herself. Angel swung the pack around and faced the steps in order to finish with the buckle. "I hope we don't need anything else from this damned pack," she said, spittle running from her lower lip. Another scream from above shook her. She shoved the pack at his back. "I can't close it!"

"It's okay. As long as I stay upright, we won't lose anything."

She held the pack while he slipped his arms into the straps. "Hurry, Kevin," she pleaded.

Still another door opened above. Kevin stepped into the basement, pivoting left and right. Nothing jumped out.

"Come on," he said. Angel stood transfixed, her gaze on the stairway. The sound of scuffling feet sliding down the cement stairs paralyzed her. He grabbed her by the back of the collar, dragged her into the basement and slammed the door. He ran the flashlight beam over the doorframe. "I thought they had a latch," he muttered. "Oh well, it doesn't matter. The dead don't have keys."

He aimed the flashlight into the recesses of the mechanical room. The dark swallowed the beam, yielding the outline of the furnace and ductwork and little else. "I can't see," she said. Her thin whisper slipped into the inky corners of the basement, disappearing like the beam.

"We need to go." He fumbled for her hand and pulled her forward.

"Where are we going?"

"Up and out." He took a few steps and then lurched forward, stumbling. "What is it?" she cried.

"Watch your step. There are boxes all over the floor."

"How can you see?" she asked. "That flashlight isn't worth a damn."

Something hammered at the door behind them.

Angel shuddered. Kevin grabbed her hand again. "It's a metal door," he reminded her, his voice almost conversational. "I came down here about a week ago, so I know where everything is. I hate the way they stowed so much crap down here, though. There are plenty of empty apartments they could have used."

"Our apartment will be empty now."

"Yes it will." Far ahead, past a huge water heater tank and more air ducts, she saw a soft glow coming from above. "See that light?" he asked. "It's an access grate. There's a ladder in the wall there. We climb up and out and we're on our way." His flashlight beam moved from side to side, then across the floor, looking for boxes they might trip over or intruders who might stumble out, mouths open and hands outstretched. The pounding on the door continued behind them.

At the base of the promised ladder, Angel looked up, expecting—and dreading—the sight of shamblers, feet on the metal grate. Instead, she saw blue sky, brushed with cloud wisps.

The ladder consisted of metal rungs fixed to the concrete wall. "Wait here," Kevin said, handing her the flashlight. He shrugged out of his pack and strapped the top closed. Then, pack on his shoulders again, he grabbed a rung and pulled himself up. The weight of the pack made his climb awkward. When he reached the top, he let go with his free hand and pushed at the grating overhead. It didn't budge. His gun hand slipped, and he grabbed frantically at the rung with his free hand. He clutched the ladder, pressing his body to the wall until he'd steadied himself.

Angel panned the room below with the flashlight. Under the open sky, the flashlight's beam seemed even dimmer. If something came lumbering at her out of the corners, would she have time to see it? She heard a sound behind her and whirled, gun extended. She couldn't see a thing.

Kevin tried the grate again, reluctant to pound at the metal grid and attract attention. He stopped, shook his head and leaned out, fumbling with a latch that held the grate in place. This time when he pushed, the metal gave way with a screech. "Come on up!" he called, trying not to shout.

He shoved at the grate, heaving it aside. In the same motion, he pitched up on the walkway, bracing himself with his gun hand.

The grate crashed against the cement walkway, attracting the attention of a man standing just a few yards behind. Kevin scrambled to his feet, but the weight of his pack threatened to send him tumbling back into the hole. He righted himself just as Angel poked her head up over the edge. "Kevin!" she warned.

The shambler wore a blue suit and tie, coated in layers of blood that had spilled and clotted. Kevin fired once, striking the man in the sternum, knocking him back two steps. Somehow, the shambler kept his feet and moved forward again, but by then Kevin had drawn careful aim. The second shot struck the thing in the forehead, blowing away the back of its skull. One piece struck the apartment building behind them. Another struck the edge of the walkway and slid off into the grass. The shambler dropped to its knees and fell face forward into the open hole where the grate had been.

The shots drew other shamblers. Kevin grabbed Angel's hand and dragged her away, walking briskly. Dozens of them—dozens!— were about to converge. Angel started to run, but Kevin held her back. "Walk," he commanded. "We can walk out of here. Save your energy."

Angel suppressed the urge to race away, or worse, stand still and scream. Ahead, shamblers turned and stared, as if trying to process the sight of a man and woman power-walking across the grass. Behind, grasping hands clutched the air. A dozen shamblers stumbled after them, a distinctive death rattle sounding in their throats.

"We're going the wrong way!" she moaned.

"We can circle around." They had crossed the length of the basement and come up on the east side of the apartment building. They needed to move west, to the foothills. Going east, into town, would be suicide.

"Do you still have the flashlight?" Kevin asked.

"I had it! I must have dropped it!"

He glanced back. "You have the gun, don't you?"

She waved it. "I'm so sorry about the flashlight!"

"Forget it," he said, pulling her into the street. "We'll get another later on." The shamblers had fallen behind. The ones in the rear had already lost interest and wandered away. Kevin could have shot the few who were left, but he'd have attracted more attention. "Keep moving," he said. "They'll give up soon."

But two of the shamblers pressed on. One was a teenaged girl, with braided hair and a broken arm that dangled like a pendulum. The other was a man in his early twenties with a goatee and a missing eye. His chest and tee shirt had been torn open. The two shamblers appeared fresh, which explained their quicker strides. Even so, Kevin and Angel had increased their lead without running.

On the backside of the apartment, Angel saw the stairwell, an enclosed concrete column attached to the outside of the building. The plywood boards had been shattered and pulled aside—a gaping hole for the shamblers to enter. She stared in horror at the door, and shook her head. If they'd stayed, they'd have been trapped. Or worse.

"They got in through the stairwell, Kevin."

"It doesn't matter. They were already in. Somebody on the fifth floor died, and that was that." Kevin removed the box of cartridges from his jeans pocket and reloaded his pistol as he walked.

"You're running out of ammo."

"We have plenty. And we haven't even fired your gun."

"What now?"

"We go to the mountains. The foothills are four miles away. We'll go straight up Mulberry to Overland Trail. Then we'll head towards the stadium and into Horsetooth Reservoir. There are places to hide on the backside of the reservoir."

"I lost the flashlight. We have to be there before dark."

Kevin smiled. "Hell, we're nearly there now, and it's not even noon."

"The sun goes down by six," she said. She wished it were summer, not March. The sun was their ally. To either side, shamblers turned to watch them as they hurried down the streets of Fort Collins.

"Be glad we're in Colorado," he said. "If we were in Iowa, the mountains would be about eight hundred miles away."

"Funny," she said, thinking that he was not funny at all. It killed her to see him smile as if they were out for a stroll instead of a death march. It was an act. If he faltered here in the streets and gave way to despair, she would put the barrel of the .32 under her chin and put a bullet in her head. If the shamblers still wanted body, they could have it. She would already be gone.

Or would she? The shamblers weren't entirely brainless. They knew to gather at a door, and if the door were unlocked, they would eventually open it. Did their rotting minds still function? And if the mind was still working on some small level, was the soul then trapped inside? She shook with revulsion. To be one of them would be worse than death, worse than being torn apart or eaten alive.

They walked west up Mulberry. Abandoned cars pocked the street. Shamblers crossed in front and behind, and a few tried to follow, but Kevin pushed the pace. Angel kept her gaze fixed on his back as she walked. The weight of the pack bothered her, and by the time they reached Shields, the first major north-south intersection, her shoulders were screaming. "Can we stop to rest?" she asked.

"There's no safe place."

She hunched over, her hands on her knees. *I'm going to vomit,* she thought. He stepped behind her and grabbed hold of the pack. "Unstrap," he ordered.

"I'm fine."

"We have a long way to go. Let me carry this. You'll be rested when I give it back. Hurry, we only have a moment."

She unbuckled her shoulder straps and slipped out of the pack. The relief was so great, she nearly cried. Kevin hoisted the pack over his shoulder, carrying it by the frame. Two shamblers had closed to within a few yards of them. Angel fought the urge to run. Her back ached as they walked. Her legs ached. "I'm so out of shape," she moaned.

"Me too. It didn't do us any good to sit in that apartment for two months."

An old man with a mottled, burgundy beard stumbled after them. He'd been dead for a while. His skin smelled of fish and rot. He staggered on thin, bandy legs, jerking with the effort to stay upright. Angel heard the man's rattle—the staccato sound of air forced past the vocal chords in stuttering bursts. His eyes had begun to recede. His mouth opened and closed as he followed, as if he could already taste them.

The intersection of Shields and Mulberry was a mess of abandoned vehicles. An SUV had climbed up over the top of a Saturn wagon, coming to rest on the windshield, crushing the roof of the tiny green wagon into the seats. A little girl, dead, peered out of the back of the wagon, her eyes like poached eggs under a tangle of black hair. She leaned forward with her face to the glass. Angel tried not to look inside as they passed. She couldn't bear the images of carnage. One glance back told her that the old man was still following them.

Kevin paused every few steps. Angel wondered if he intended to commandeer one of the vehicles and drive to the mountains, but Mulberry was a clutter of wrecks as far west as she could see. No one could drive this road.

Kevin stopped in front of a Volvo and looked into the windows. The car was empty. "These folks left home without packing anything!" To the left and right, shamblers converged on them, stumbling through the maze of abandoned cars.

"Kevin?"

"I know," he said. "But you never know what you'll find."

"They're everywhere!"

"They'll thin out when we get to the mountains," he promised. "We're still in town. The college owns half of Overland Trail. There's nothing but research buildings and open fields. Once we get there, it won't be like this. " He circled left around the Volvo and slid between two pickup trucks. A shambler stepped into the space ahead, and Kevin fired the Ruger, blowing an ear off, but not putting it down. His second shot shattered the thing's head. Kevin moved forward, cursing. He slid past the pickups and paused to plot his next move. The sound of gunfire drew the attention of the shamblers at the edge of the road. A woman in a nightgown turned and raised her one remaining arm, pointing it at them.

"Run now," Kevin said, hustling between the cars, weaving his way past Toyotas and Fords, the extra pack banging off car windows and side view mirrors. Angel ran to the sound of a scream, not realizing at first that it was her own cry spilling out.

Kevin fired the Ruger and then fired again. He moved north now, weaving his way to the open grass of City Park. He did not glance back, not even to check on her, a realization that chilled her as nothing else had. Clumps of red littered the park grass. Some of the piles throbbed, and some were silent and still, like flesh markers in a carnival graveyard. Angel nearly stumbled, but kept her feet as she moved on, racing past the outstretched hands and the empty eyes.

Just when she thought she could go no further, Kevin grabbed her by the arm, pulling her to a stop. She gasped, sucking in huge lungfulls of air. "I can't breathe."

"We're all right for a moment." A pair of shamblers eyed them from a short distance, but hadn't begun to pursue. He pulled the ammo box from his jeans and reloaded the Ruger. "We can walk now."

"Let's stay off the road," she said.

He laughed. "Good idea."

How can he laugh? She bent over, nearly vomiting. "I'm . . . out of . . .shape."

"Come on," he said. "They're moving again." He shoved the ammo box into his jeans pocket and turned west. "Walk, don't run."

Her ankles throbbed. They had only gone a third of the way to safety. She flinched at the word. There was no safety to be found. "Where are we going to stay tonight?"

"I don't know yet," he said. "Are you okay?"

"Fine," she said, nearly overwhelmed with the enormity of the lie.

They stayed off the pavement, avoiding the tangles of lost cars and trucks. The park grass took them nearly to Taft Hill Road. From there, they would have to return to the street, but hopefully, traffic would thin out as they approached the foothills.

One station wagon, luggage covering a roof rack, caught their attention. "Let me check this," he told her. She waited from a distance. *There are children inside that car.*

Kevin glanced back and saw her expression. "There are a lot of them in the cars we just passed," he said. "They get bitten or scratched or just get left behind. There's nothing we can do." His expression hardened. "It's important you understand. They aren't children anymore."

"How do you know?" she asked. She stepped closer and looked. There were two inside. A girl with straight blond hair, perhaps six or seven years old, threw herself at the window, leaving bloody smears on the inside glass. In the backseat, a baby lay strapped inside a car seat. The baby's face had been eaten. It moved suddenly, tiny arms thrashing, legs kicking. Then it lay still.

"Oh," Angel said, and sat down on the grass. "Oh."

"They're not children," Kevin repeated from the top of the wagon, sorting through the luggage. After a few moments, he hopped down and pulled Angel to her feet. "Come on," he demanded. "Let's go."

She almost told him no. The urge to quit was strong. But she began to walk, and he gave her a wavering smile, nearly sick with relief. She suddenly realized that if she hadn't been with him, he'd have taken his own life by now. The despair in his blue eyes gave him away. He could only pretend so far. *A fine pair we are,* she thought.

She felt the wet, spongy grass give beneath her feet as they walked. She could smell fresh blossoms in the air. The trees had sprouted leaves. Kevin had said that when the hot days of summer came, the shamblers would rot and disintegrate, and the crisis would be over. The thought of waiting for three or four months to find out if he was right was unbearable.

She stared at him again, stumbling along with two packs and a gun. Could she really take her own life? No, not now, not with the sun directly overhead, a white light that almost made her smile.

But if she'd had to face this ordeal at dawn, she'd have already pulled the trigger.

Her doctor called her illness "melancholia," a form of depression. The symptoms included early-morning sorrow, often triggered by the sight of the rising sun, a loss of appetite and weight and an emotional withdrawal from close relationships. The last symptom was problematic. She cared for Kevin and did her best to show him. She had to, if she wanted to survive.

She approached each morning with a sense of dread. In a perfect world, she might sleep late. The sun would be overhead—like it was now—when she woke, and she would escape the crushing despair that ate her alive.

Instead, she woke most mornings before sunrise, her sense of dread compounded exponentially by the shuffling dead outside her window.

Now she raced along Mulberry Street, weaving through wrecked cars, past splashed blood and chunks of flesh and bone, neglected lawns, animated corpses and traffic lights that had gone out forever. A sudden flush of emotion threatened to cripple her. A glance to either sidewalk reminded her that the world had gone crazy, and everyone in it was doomed.

To the right, a fat woman, forever barefoot, struggled after them, running into a row of shrubs, twisting through the brambles, her cotton dress tearing, leaving strips of yellow cloth on the branches like streamers.

To the left, two young boys no more than ten years old stood open-mouthed, staring at the sun. One was naked from the waist down, his legs encrusted with dried mud. As Kevin and Angel passed, they looked away from the sky with sun-fried sockets, unable to see. The one with clothing sniffed the air, and began to follow.

In the distance, Mulberry ended in a T-intersection with the actual site of the historic Overland Trail, the route west during the pioneer days. The street was jammed full of cars, SUVs and pickups. *Are there no empty roads left?*

Kevin stopped at a pile of bones and cloth, clotted in brown. There was no flesh left, no muscle—nothing to reanimate. Nearby, a pile of black liquid coated the end of a driveway. The smell was overpowering, as if feces and vomit had been boiled down to a paste. Angel retched, though there was nothing in her stomach left to come up. "My God," she moaned. "What is it? Did one of them dissolve or something?"

Kevin looked back at her and shrugged, his eyes narrow and unreadable. "Come on. We need to keep moving."

"Kevin, I have to go to the bathroom."

"Me too. But not here. It smells." He waved her on, the gun in one hand, the second backpack in the other.

She dragged herself forward, her eyes locked on his back, forcing one foot in front of the other, trying not to think about her bladder. It was difficult. Though he had both packs, she was carrying a load of her own. After all, he wasn't pregnant.

When they reached the T-intersection, Kevin paused. An unending line of cars glutted the road south. Kevin's face sagged. Sweat ran down his round cheeks, his eyes red at the rims. "Every car on the planet stopped here!" he said, pointing at the jumble of vehicles that blocked the streets, the sidewalks and the fields.

"Everyone headed for the mountains," Angel mumbled.

Kevin set the backpack down and put his hands on his hips. *We can't just follow the herd,* he thought. *The herd is dead, looking for food.* He tried to think, to reason. Nothing came to him. *She's waiting for me to decide. She's counting on me!* He turned to Angel and tried to smile. "My back is sore. I need to rest a minute."

A shambler made its way toward them from across the street, step by halting step.

"You're carrying my pack. It's too much."

"You'll get it back when I get tired."

Angel grabbed for the pack, but he moved it out of her reach.

"I'm fine," he insisted. "I just need a moment." He pointed his gun over her shoulder. "You've got one coming up behind you."

Angel whirled. The shambler wore a basketball jersey and a pair of nylon shorts. His right leg was broken at the top of the shin, bone poking through the gray flesh. With each step, the bone cut through muscle and skin, splintering with the stress, finally tearing free, sending him tumbling to the street. The shambler lay still for a moment and then crawled forward, pulling himself by the fingertips toward Kevin and Angel. His mouth worked like a fish in an aquarium.

"Let's go," Kevin said. He tried to hide the panic in his voice.

"North or south?"

I can't think!

Across the road, beyond the cars, Kevin saw a building, surrounded by chain link topped with security wire. A trim, black woman in a blue uniform stood looking at him, her arms folded, a pistol in her hand.

"There," Kevin said, pointing.

They wound their way through the maze of cars, each turn a danger, watching for the sudden grasp and bite of someone under a car or between cars. When they reached the lawn, Kevin called out. "Hello!"

No answer.

"We're headed for Disneyland, and I think we took a wrong turn."

The black woman shook her head.

Kevin looked at Angel. Her eyes had that haunted look that came in the early morning. "Say," he called out. "Any vacancies in there?" He glanced behind. Two more shamblers headed their way.

"What kind of pistol is that?" the woman asked in a crisp, businesslike voice.

"Ruger, .44-caliber, stainless steel barrel. You can wash it in the sink."

She nodded. "What's the girl got?"

"A .32."

"Ammo?"

"Some. You taking inventory?"

The woman flashed a sardonic smile, a slow twist of the lips. "You're drawing a crowd," she said. Another shambler had joined the first two, less than twenty feet away now.

"You going to let us in?"

The black woman stared.

"Please!" Angel called, her voice breaking.

The woman nodded. "Come around back. There's a gate in the rear. Run. I don't want these fuckers to figure out where the door is."

Kevin grabbed Angel's arm and pulled her forward. She stumbled and then raced beside him, tracing the perimeter of the fence. The foothills loomed to the west, across the field. They rounded the fence corner and headed for the gate while the black woman fumbled with the lock. A shambler rounded the opposite corner from the north, sixty feet in front of them, pulling himself along the chain link.

Kevin reached the gate before the shambler, but the woman hadn't yet opened the lock. He raised the Ruger and fired point blank, knocking the shambler into the wet grass.

The black woman jumped and looked up. "That's fucking noisy," she said.

"Hurry, please!" Angel cried.

The lock popped. The woman pulled the gate open. Kevin pushed Angel inside and followed. The black woman shoved the gate closed and reset the lock. Several shamblers had followed at the edge of the fence, and though they were close enough for Kevin to hear their breathy rattle, they would not get inside. He turned and faced the woman. Her gaze jumped back and forth from Kevin to Angel to the shamblers.

For a moment, no one said anything. Kevin smiled, tucked the gun under his arm and held out a hand. "My name's Kevin. This is Angel. Thank you for saving us."

The woman's eyes settled, and she took Kevin's hand. "Janet. Janet Atwood. I see you can use that Ruger."

Kevin shrugged. "Point and shoot."

Janet gave him the sardonic smile again. She looked pretty in an unconventional way, her hair pulled back in a frizzy ponytail, brown eyes taking over the rest of her angular face. She wore a security guard's uniform, her name embroidered on the front. She was slender, but her arms were taut with lean muscle. She carried her weapon as though it were an extension of her fist.

"What's the building?" he asked. "Are you alone here?"

"It's part of the college," she answered. "It's a research facility. They used to study pine beetles here. Now they study zombies. Come on. I'll introduce you to the others."

They headed for the door, a metal entry with a small window. An unhappy face pressed against the glass from the inside. Kevin wondered how welcome they'd be.

"It's okay," Janet called. "They're cool. Open up."

The door cracked open, six inches—no more. Someone spoke to Janet in a forced whisper. She pushed at the door. "Open up, God damn it!" After a pause, the door swung open.

A thin man peered out, shaken and pale. He wore a student's clothing—a ball cap with the bill pointed off to the side, jeans with a pair of gym shorts pulled over them and a Marilyn Manson tee shirt. But his face told a different story. Crow's feet and stubble aged him.

"What the fuck, Janet?" Bernard whispered, as if Kevin and Angel couldn't hear him.

"I'm not going to leave them out there, Bernard," she said, stressing his name as if it were a pejorative. She swept him aside with her arm.

Fluorescents lit the inside of the building. "You have electricity?" Kevin asked, awe in his voice.

"Hell yeah," Janet said. "Fuel tank out back, generators in the maintenance room."

"Atwood!" Bernard moaned.

"They're not here to harm anyone, Bernard. They're here to rest without being killed."

Bernard shook his head and retreated down the hall.

"This is one of those labs I mentioned," Kevin whispered. "That's pretty convenient."

Janet heard him and answered, "This is university land. There are two other labs on this street alone."

Others joined them in the lobby of the building—a mix of young and old, women and men. There were no children. They greeted Kevin and Angel with outstretched arms and wide, open-mouthed smiles. Kevin felt someone grab his hand and shake it, and the touch was so welcome, he felt the onset of tears. The sudden rush of emotion embarrassed him.

"And who is this?" A thin, gray-haired woman stepped forward, hands clasped at her stomach, feet together, back straight, her head cocked to the side.

"Kevin Brown and Angel Hess," Kevin said. "This gal here was kind enough to let us in." He raised the Ruger and then, blushing, pointed the gun back down at the floor. "Sorry," he whispered.

"Maybe you should give the gun to Ms. Atwood," the gray-haired woman said with a faint smile. "We don't allow guns inside the facility, except for Janet's of course. She's in charge of security. She'll return the gun to you when you leave."

Kevin hesitated, but Angel stepped in front of him and handed Janet the .32, butt first. Kevin surrendered the Ruger a moment later.

"Thank you," the gray-haired woman said. She repositioned herself, feet apart. "My name is Candice Paulsen. I'm the unofficial director of this facility. You are welcome here. I'm sorry if it seems like we're mobbing you, but we don't get visitors. Not ones we like anyway." She smiled, but the joke fell flat.

Angel leaned against the wall, her legs crossed. "I'm sorry, but I need to use a toilet. Now."

"Of course," Candice said. "Follow me."

Kevin followed. "Are there two bathrooms? I'm ready to burst myself."

Candice took Angel's arm. "Just one bathroom per floor. This is a research facility."

What, scientists don't piss?

Kevin let Angel go first. Candice waited, silent. I don't think she trusts me, Kevin thought.

"I'm sorry if it seems like I don't trust you," Candice said at last. "But we have various projects underway here, and we've just met."

"Your hospitality is appreciated," Kevin assured her.

When both Kevin and Angel had relieved themselves, Candice led them back to the lobby. Smiling faces greeted them and Angel tried to return the hellos, but her faltering steps gave away her fatigue. "Is there a place we can rest for an hour or two?" Kevin asked. "We've been on the run for most of the day."

"Oh my, of course," Candice said. "Corey, would you take these two nice people downstairs to one of the offices?" A man standing next to Janet at the door nodded. Candice turned to Angel. "I'll have someone bring you some blankets. There aren't any beds, I'm afraid, but the floor is carpeted, so it's warm."

"That would be wonderful," Angel sighed.

"Corey, you'll scare up some blankets, won't you?"

"Sure." Corey led them down a short hall, past computer terminals and a workstation, to the stairway. A buzz of conversation followed them as they left.

The basement was a cluster of file cabinets, photocopy machines, a computer terminal and worktables. Small offices surrounded the work area. "Are all of these offices empty?" Kevin asked.

"No," Corey said, pointing at an office behind the stairs. "That's where I sleep."

"How many people live here?" Angel asked.

Corey smiled. "There are ten of us." He grabbed the last blanket from under the stairs and led them to a corner office. "This one is nice. Go on in. It's not locked."

Kevin opened the door and peered in. The room had a small desk and an empty bookshelf. He turned back. "This is great. Thank you." He held out a hand. "My name's Kevin. Kevin Brown."

Corey grabbed the hand and shook it. "Corey Singleton." His voice was strong and clear, as if he were introducing a guest speaker.

Kevin motioned to Angel. "And this is Angel."

Angel took his hand and tried to smile. Her eyes drooped and the corners of her mouth trembled.

"You're tired," Corey said. "I'll leave you alone." He took a step away. "Oh, there is one thing. Please don't go exploring, okay? We're trying to find out what caused all of this. Some of the research is sensitive. You know, fragile? Tissue samples, that sort of thing. When you wake up, just come on upstairs and find Candice or me. Is that okay?"

"Sure," Kevin said, anxious to get inside the room. Angel looked ready to collapse.

"Really," Corey said. "You could fuck something up if you went in the wrong room."

Kevin pulled Angel into the room. "We're not going anywhere but here." His voice was polite, but clipped. Angel continued into the room, dragging him by the hand.

"All right then," Corey smiled, handing over the blanket.

Kevin closed the door and exhaled. Angel stood with her back to him, her arms folded, staring at the small window at the top of the back wall. Weeds and dirt covered the view. Kevin put a gentle hand on her shoulder.

"I don't like basement windows," she said. "Things can get in."

"I like them just fine. People can get out." He propped both backpacks against the wall, glad to be free of the burden.

She shook her head. "There's nowhere safe."

"Let it go for a few hours, Angel."

She turned and slipped into his arm. He led her to the corner, lay her down on the floor and covered her with the blanket. "A nap will do us both good." He nestled close, arms around her.

"Are you comfortable?" he asked.

She nodded against his chest.

He closed his eyes and tried to relax.

<hr>

They sat in a circle so everyone would have an equal place in the discussion, but the other nine people deferred to Candice, shifting unconsciously to face her at the top of the circle. She sat still, head cocked to listen. When someone spoke, she turned, eyes locked without blinking. Her expression carried a hint of sadness.

"One important issue is food," Roger Coleman said. He was a tall

31

man with a frosted beard and balding head, distinguished and even handsome for a man in his early sixties. Coleman was the viral expert in the small community. "We're eating Ramen now. Tomorrow, we'll be eating the wrappers."

Charles Broderick was a minister who had been visiting the University when the outbreak began. He was a thin man, getting thinner, wracked by insomnia and unable to eat. Dark circles rimmed his eyes, and though his voice still held a hint of the deep, sonorous tones he'd once used in a church, the others in the circle were reluctant to meet his sunken gaze. "If we send them back out, they will die. Let's not mistake that."

Candice nodded, almost imperceptibly, though several of the others took note.

"They seem like nice folks," Corey said.

Wanda McIntyre shook her head, whipping her straight brown hair from side to side. "They are nice. Everyone's nice. But we have a team here, and the question is, do these two people have anything to offer?" It seemed like Corey wanted to speak again, so she forged ahead. "They aren't scientists," she paused to glance at the minister, "or experts in any field. They're just two people who want our food."

Bernard Wilkins was the group's computer expert. He sat shivering, a tic he'd acquired in recent weeks. He chewed at a fingernail and then wiped his hand on his tee shirt across Marilyn Manson's face. "I worry about the food thing. I mean, I guess I agree with Wanda."

Corey jumped in. "I need help," he said. "Since Big Tom joined the other side, I'm one person short on my project. As you all know, it's not a one-person project." Jason Brock, astronomer, addressed Candice directly. "If nothing else, the girl could help in the kitchen. I'll bet Trudy is sick of doing all the work in there." Trudy nodded. "The thing is, I thought we were going to be different. I thought we were going to avoid the old mistakes, the ones that caused all of this. Is that true, or is it just bullshit?" Jason looked around the circle, his long lashes lowered for a moment. He scratched his chin stubble and smiled. "If we're going to break the patterns of the past, if we're going to be the people we said we'd be, the people we should have been but never were, then we can't send these two people out in the cold. We just can't do it."

Candice nodded, smiling, her eyes shining.

"But what about the food?" Todd Smith said. He tugged at the collar of his Hawaiian shirt and looked up again. His licked his lips. "We're nearly out of food." Before the dead began to rise, Todd had been an associate professor in the Cultural Studies Department at the university.

Janet Atwood stood at the door, staring through the small window at the dead that had gathered by the gate. "He can use a gun," she said. "He had to shoot one of them to get in. He didn't blink." The observation silenced the discussion.

After a few moments, Corey spoke again. "So how about this? The guy works with me and with Janet too. And he's got to forage for supplies."

"You want to send him out alone for food?" Janet asked.

"I guess that wouldn't work, would it?" Corey said.

"Sure it would," Bernard said. "He'd have to leave the girl behind, of course. That would ensure that he'd come back."

Jason scowled. "What are you thinking? We don't hold hostages!"

"I'd go with him," Janet said.

"What?"

"I'd go out with him. To find food, and to find—"

Candice interrupted, her smile gone. "That simply will not do." Her voice had taken on a sterner, matronly tone. "You are in charge of security here at the facility. Perhaps the young man, Kevin, wouldn't mind going out alone. Or perhaps we'll have another volunteer."

"If you send any of us out," Todd said, pulling at the tangles in his unkempt beard, "then you put a research project at risk. None of us can be spared."

"Send Trudy then," Janet scoffed. Trudy's face nearly dissolved into tears. "I'm kidding, Trudy!" Janet said. "I'm just trying to make a point."

"We could send them both," Bernard said. "The guy and his girlfriend."

Jason shook his head. "Are you listening to yourself?"

"What if these people hadn't shown up?" Janet asked, but other voices trampled her words. She repeated herself in a louder, angrier voice. "What would you have done if these people had never shown up? Who did you imagine was going to go for food?"

"You," Wanda said. "I'm not afraid to say it. You would have had to go, sooner or later."

Janet shrugged as if the problem were solved. "Then I'll go with the new guy and everything will be fine."

"That won't do," Candice repeated. Her face went blank, and her voice quivered.

"What do you suggest then? We need supplies. We need food. We need medicine." Janet paused, turning to Candice. "And we need—"

"Wait a minute," Corey said, grinning. "Listen to us! We aren't arguing anymore about whether or not they should stay. We're arguing about what they should do and who's going to help them do it. We've already decided, haven't we? As for who does what, we can figure that out later, right?"

"Shall we vote?" Candice asked with an air of finality. The others nodded. Candice raised a hand. "Who votes for having them stay?" Corey's hand shot up. Janet and the minister raised their hands as well. When a few more hands joined in, even Bernard and Rod voted yes. "It's unanimous," Candice smiled. Bernard started to stand up, but she motioned him to wait.

"I want to say something now," she announced. She waited until Bernard sat back in the circle to continue. "This was an important vote. More than that, I believe with all my heart that this was a test. We are people with both hearts and minds. But if our hearts are found wanting, what good are our minds?

"We're doing important work here," she continued. "We all have important roles. But the most important task each of us has is to be a human being first. When we came together as a group, we agreed that the old ways weren't going to work here. The reminders of humanity's past mistakes are standing outside at the fence, waiting to get in." Now her voice broke with emotion, and her hands trembled. "We are not the only research facility left. I believe that with all my heart. But we have to act as if we were. We have to act as if we were the last people on the planet. We are a family. And if the end of humanity is here, then we must face it doing the right things for the right reasons."

"I'm fine with that," Rod said. "And we're trying. But humanity has to eat." He punctuated the end of his sentence with a nervous laugh, glancing around for validation. No one met his gaze. "Am I wrong?"

"I think these new people might be more of a solution than a problem," Candice said, her voice smooth again. Rod's shoulders slumped.

"So, do I have a new partner?"

Candice pretended to be angry. "Corey, you are incorrigible!" Then she nodded. "Yes. It's time to get your project going again."

When Angel stirred, Kevin slid out from under her arm and crept to the door, hoping she might go back to sleep. *No such luck for me,* he thought. When he opened the door, he found Corey waiting for him.

"Hey! Did you get some rest?"

Kevin stared, his hand still on the doorknob. "Have you been waiting here all this time?"

Corey smiled. "No, not at all."

"I just woke up. Thanks for letting us rest." He glanced back at Angel as he closed the door, and then turned to face Corey. *This guy is lying. He's been there the whole time.* Kevin kept his face blank. "So, what now?"

Corey's smile widened. "Why? You got a plane to catch?" Kevin didn't answer. "Hey, lighten up, okay? The good news is we want you to stay. You and the girl. How does that sound?"

Kevin nodded. "What's the bad news?"

"We're surrounded by zombies."

"Funny," Kevin said.

"Yeah. Here's the real bad news; you have to work with me." Kevin pressed his lips together. "I'm not cracking you up, am I? Let me start over. We're working on various projects. My project requires two guys, and my partner, well he's dead." His voice dropped away to a whisper. "He's one of them now."

"What do you mean by project?"

Corey stepped back and grabbed a chair from the workstation in the center of the room. "You have a second?"

Kevin didn't move.

"Everyone here is attacking the zombie problem from a different point of view. My project is field research. The zombies are dead, right? And they're rotting. Some of them look like hell. Some of them are fresh." Corey leaned forward in the chair, his hands on his knees. "But does anyone know how long it will take for them to rot away? To stop being a threat?"

"That's something I've wondered."

"We're scientists here—most of us, anyway. My specialty before the Apocalypse was wildlife. I was working on my Masters when everything went to hell. As a scientist, I want to approach the question systematically. So I worked up a method of tracking the rot, so to speak."

"How?"

"Catch and release," Corey said, a goofy smile on his face. "Sounds crazy, right? I catch them, tag them and send them back out. When I come across a tagged specimen, I make specific notes about the decay, how fast a zombie moves, how it's functioning."

"You tag them," Kevin said dully.

Corey tapped his shirt collar with his index finger. "I staple them with a numbered tag. Cool, eh?"

Candice handed Angel a bowl of Ramen, fortified with tiny cuts of chicken and vegetables. "It's not much, but we find we can get along without eating as much as in the past. My father used to say that most people 'dig a grave with their teeth.' I can't disagree."

"Any hot food is a blessing," Angel said. "We've been eating granola bars and graham crackers for weeks."

"Oh my," Candice said, shaking her head. "All that processed sugar. You must feel awful."

Angel gave a self-conscious laugh. *In a world overrun by the dead, processed sugar is not a tragedy.*

"You'll find that we eat as healthy as possible here," Candice said. "This brand of noodles was air-dried, not fried. And the vegetables are fresh. We have a small greenhouse garden out in the compound. We don't spend much time out there, of course. We don't want to attract attention. But Trudy goes out once a day to water and weed. It's good to eat fresh!"

Angel sat at a table in the ground floor dining room. Most of the others had eaten already. Corey and Kevin sat alone, focusing on their soup. Candice stood, arms folded, watching Angel eat.

"Aren't you going to join us?" Angel asked.

"No, you take your time. When you're finished, we can talk."

Kevin pushed his bowl away. Corey slurped down the last of his soup and pushed his bowl next to Kevin's.

Why is she staring at me? Am I supposed to stop eating? Angel took another bite, a string of noodles hanging from her chin. She blushed and pushed the food into her mouth.

"No one can eat Ramen gracefully," Kevin observed.

Angel placed her unfinished bowl a few inches closer to the center of the table. "I don't want you to have to wait for me," she said. "What do you want to talk about?"

Candice smiled and sat down, putting a hand on Angel's knee. "What are your plans? Do you have a destination in mind?"

"No," she whispered.

"I only ask because so many of us talk about going home and finding out what happened to our families. Some of our original team actually tried that. Who knows where they are now? But for the ones who've stayed, this is their family."

"My family is gone," Angel said.

"Then let me suggest something to you," Candice said. "You and your friend should consider staying with us."

"I told them," Corey said.

Candice frowned.

"I mean I told him," Corey said, pointing to Kevin.

Candice shifted her chair and took Angel's hand. "Well then, what do you think? Would you like to stay with all of us?"

Angel looked at Kevin. He shrugged, smiling. She turned back. "I'd love it."

"Good," Candice said. "I hope Kirk approves."

"Kevin."

"I'm sorry," Candice said, a hint of a blush. "Kevin. Well Kevin, I don't know how much Corey told you, but let me fill you in on the facility. This structure has a ground floor and a basement. You've seen the basement, of course. There's also a ladder to the roof in the maintenance room." She pointed behind her. "We think of the roof as our final defense in the event of a security breach."

Kevin nodded, his face a blank.

"This is a research facility," Candice continued. "There are several labs and several computer workstations. We have our own server here, so we're still able to contact other computers."

"You're in contact with other survivors?" Kevin sat forward, his eyes narrowed.

"No, not per se," Candice answered. Her eyes turned down and her smile disappeared. "Most Internet servers are down. The government has sites up, but they haven't been updated for a week or two. We've tried to contact other people around the country, but we haven't connected with anyone recently. We will, though.

"At any rate," she continued, "we had supplies and a secure workplace, so we went about trying to find an answer to the . . . problem. It spread so quickly! No time to discover the cause. That's what we're doing here. We're searching for the cause."

"If the government is still operating, won't they do the same?"

"Oh, I hope so!" Candice said. "But in the meantime, we're working at the problem from several angles."

"It's a shotgun approach," Corey added. "If one idea doesn't work, another might."

Candice smiled in agreement. "Of course, if you decide to stay, you'll be asked to carry your share of the workload."

"I'm not a scientist," Angel said, thinking, *I'm an office manager.*

"I know, dear, but there are other things to do. Trudy has been stuck with the cooking and cleaning—a clean lab is a must—and she could use some help. And Corey expressed an interest in having Kevin assist him with his project."

Angel glanced to Kevin again, and when he nodded, she said, "We'd be glad for the work."

Candice sat back. "Well! That's wonderful." She paused, glancing at Corey. "Did you explain our rules?"

"Nope."

"What kind of rules?" Kevin asked.

Candice tilted her head. "Let me ask you: have you wondered why this all happened? Why the world ended? Not the cause of the plague, if that's what it is. The cause behind the cause." She paused to sigh. "The human race has not done a good job with the gift of life. We destroy. We pollute. We hurt each other and we hurt the planet. Would you agree?"

Angel nodded. Kevin sat without moving.

"When we came together here, we decided to live as if this was the last outpost of humankind. We want to avoid the mistakes of the past. We don't accumulate personal belongings. We eat and drink in moderation. We don't waste things. We reuse them. And we treat each other with compassion. We are a family. If this is where humanity's story ends, we will write a bittersweet epilogue."

Angel was touched by the poetry in her voice, but with a glance to the side, she caught Corey rolling his eyes. He's heard this speech before. She smiled at Candice. "That's beautiful."

Candice smiled back, her eyes closing for a brief moment, as if she'd found a kindred soul. Then she stood and turned to Kevin. "We need some help in the area of supply procurement. I'm told you're a sure hand with a gun."

It was Kevin's turn to smile.

"Along the same lines, would you please give your backpacks, along with any spare ammunition, to Janet? She's the young woman who let you in earlier this afternoon. She'll put the items in storage for everyone's use."

"Why is that?" Kevin asked.

"I mentioned that we avoid personal belongings. Whatever you need, we'll provide. Whatever you have will provide for the needs of others."

Kevin looked at Angel. "Not the teddy."

Angel's face flushed with embarrassment. Kevin could be an ass sometimes. "Yes, of course. We'll bring everything up right away."

"This is a mistake," Kevin said.

"If we want to stay, then we have to turn in our things," Angel said. "They made that clear. This is the price of admission."

He stared at the floor of their room, hands jammed in his pockets.

Angel tied off the top of her pack. "Come on. Quit pouting and help me carry these up."

"You're right," he said, not moving. "But when we hand over these things, we give up our escape plan."

"Where is there to escape to?"

"I don't know. We never even got out of town."

Angel propped the backpacks against the door. "If you want me to say no, I'll say no." She turned, arms folded. "I trust your judgment." *But I want to stay, please!*

He stood, hands on his hips. He looked into her eyes for a moment and nodded. "We're staying. But I want you to understand what's bothering me. Remember when Candice said the roof was their contingency plan? That's not a contingency plan. That's a grave. No food, no shelter, no water and no escape." He shook his head. "These people don't know a thing about defense. When we hand the backpacks over, we give up our fallback plan. We join these people on the roof."

"Then why are we staying?"

"Because I'm not dragging you out past the fence on a hunch."

"Let's give it a few days," she suggested. "If—"

The knock at the door startled her. She looked at him with a stricken expression.

"Shamblers don't knock," he said.

She shook her head at him and opened the door.

Janet Atwood stood with her arms crossed and a frown on her face. "Hey, how are you two doing?"

"Fine," Angel said. "Can I help you?"

"Candice sent me. She thought you might need help with the equipment you brought in."

"Equipment my ass," Kevin said.

Janet scowled. "Look, I keep the munitions locked up. That way, we keep a gun-free community. Believe me, it's better that way. You already handed over the handguns. You might as well give me the ammunition and let us keep it safe for you."

"Thanks for that," Kevin said, his voice tainted with sarcasm. He crossed the room, pulled the box of bullets from the backpack and handed it to Janet.

Janet opened the box, stared at it a moment and then looked up. "What about the .32?"

"Five rounds left in the gun."

"You walked in here with two guns and twenty rounds?"

Kevin nodded.

"You're fucking kidding me," Janet said, her face twisted in disbelief. "That's all you brought us?"

"We brought granola, too," Kevin said. "You seem like you could use the fiber."

Janet's face went blank. She pursed her lips for a moment and looked down at the backpacks. "I'll take these upstairs," she said. "Can you help me with one of them?"

Kevin started to speak, but Angel interrupted. "Of course we'll help." Janet grabbed a pack. Angel grabbed the other. Together, they headed up the stairs, leaving Kevin in the doorway.

When Angel returned ten minutes later, she brought an open bottle of Budweiser with her. She crossed the room and extended the bottle. "They gave us a cold beer to share," she said. "You drink it. I'm not thirsty."

Kevin sat on the floor with his back against the wall. He took the beer, frowning. He looked at the label and then held the bottle against his cheek. "What, is this a bribe?"

"They already have our things. Just drink the beer and be grateful."

He nodded, took a sip and closed his eyes. "Oh, that's really good. I haven't had a beer in forever."

"I thought you'd like it," she said. She sat next to him and waited while he drank, leaning her head on his shoulder. He seemed to be at peace, so she was silent. After a while, he asked, "So what now?"

"We work. They want you to go with Corey when you wake up tomorrow."

"Okay."

"I guess I'm going to cook."

"Well, don't burn the Ramen."

When the sun went down, they went back upstairs. "I want to get to know everyone, and I want them to get a chance to know us," Angel said, dragging him by the hand. "Be charming."

"I am charming," he groused.

"This isn't like the apartment. You only went out to take care of residents that died. I never went out. I want to do better this time."

"You're the boss."

The residents of the lab had gathered in the lobby near the entrance. The rest of the facility was divided into labs and cubicles, or workstations like the center of the basement. The lobby had become the de facto living room for the residents. There were a few office chairs, all filled. Two women sat on a desk like cake toppers. As soon as Kevin and Angel entered the room, everyone sprang to their feet in welcome, a movement so perfectly timed it seemed rehearsed.

Candice grabbed Angel's hand and pulled her into the center of the room. She began introductions, careful to include everyone. "This is Bernard, and this is Jason, and these two young ladies are Wanda and Trudy. You'll be working with Trudy." She glanced back at Kevin with a smile. "Everyone? This is Kevin. He'll be working with Corey."

Kevin waved and joined Corey by the door while Candice swept Angel through more introductions. Kevin braced his back against the doorframe and watched.

"Everybody likes your girl," Corey noted.

"She's a nice person."

"Pretty, too."

"Yes."

"Great face. Nice body. I like slender girls. Are you guys married?"

Kevin glanced to the side, locking eyes with Corey. "No, we're not married."

"How long have you known her?"

"A year or so. She was my boss."

"No kidding? Dating the boss, huh?"

"We've only been together since the dead started walking."

Corey nodded as if that was the answer he'd expected. He looked back to Angel. She stood, arms at her sides, conversing with a good-looking man about Kevin's age. The man had expressive eyes with long lashes and the hint of a private sorrow. "Who's that?" Kevin asked.

"That's Jason, Jason Brock. He's an astronomer. I'm not surprised he's latched on to your girl. The pickings are mighty slim around here."

Kevin pointed to Wanda. "She seems attractive enough." Wanda had straight brown hair and a kewpie doll face.

"That's Wanda. She's a bitch. And I think she's gay. She and Trudy live together. They flirt with the guys, but no one's had any luck with either of them. I mean, if a girl doesn't want me, then what the hell? She's gotta be gay, you know what I mean?" He winked.

"You're kind of an idiot, aren't you?"

Corey laughed. "Jason's talking to your gal, and you're over here talking to me. Who's the idiot?"

Kevin scowled and launched himself away from the door. Candice stepped forward, taking his arm. "Can I introduce you to anyone?" she beamed.

"Sure. Where's Janet?"

Candice looked around the room. "She's not here, so she's either in her room or up on the roof. Knowing Janet, I'd bet on the roof. She sometimes stays up there all night, watching over us."

"How do I get there?"

"Go straight back, past the stairs. Go through the maintenance room door. The ladder is at the very back."

"Thank you," Kevin said. He followed her directions to the rear of the facility. The metal ladder was fixed to the wall. It reminded him of the ladder in the basement of the apartment complex. How long ago had that been? Ten hours or a hundred years? He grabbed a rung and pulled himself up.

The roof surface was flat, topped with various machines and vents. The roof was relatively new—no tar and no pools of rainwater. Janet stood at the west end of the building, elbows on the lip of the roof. Kevin scrambled through the roof hatch and joined her. Below, a dozen shamblers stood motionless near the gate, faces close to the chain link.

Janet looked at him once and then returned to her reverie.

Kevin glanced up. A low, slivered moon hung low on the horizon. With the lights of the city gone, perhaps forever, the clear, cold sky was a vast field of stars, clustered pinpricks of light so deep he felt as if he could rise into the night air and disappear. A brief moment of vertigo made him grab the lip of the roof for support.

"Quite a few of them tonight," Janet said. Her voice was soft, barely audible.

"Do they usually hover around the fence?" He kept his voice low to match hers.

Janet shook her head. "Your coming here seems to have stirred them up."

"Is that why we're whispering?"

"If I'm quiet, they never notice me. Not on the roof. They don't look up. And if they did, well, I'm too dark to see. You best keep your pasty white face out of sight."

"I have a ruddy complexion, not pasty. And I came up here to ask you about security. Am I right in thinking that the only thing between them and us is the fence?"

"This facility is all metal and brick."

"The basement floor offices have ground-level windows. No bars. Has anybody thought about securing the building?"

"Wow, that's a really great idea."

"I like sarcasm," he said. When she didn't answer, he continued. "The roof is a lousy fallback position. We get ourselves trapped up here with no water, no food, and we'll all end up shambling."

She shook her head. "It gets tiresome," she said.

He waited.

"Everybody's an expert. You've been here half a day, and you want to run security."

"I didn't say that. I said we could bar the windows."

"With what?"

He shrugged.

"No, come on. What's the great idea?"

"I don't know what materials or tools you have."

"We don't have shit."

"We could arm an expedition and go hit a hardware store or something."

She looked at him. "And who would go?"

"I would."

She snorted and looked away again. After a long pause, she said,

"I suppose you would. Well, if we could convince these people to let us go, I might take you up on that." She snorted again. "That'd teach you to open your mouth."

"I'd go tomorrow, if you asked me to."

"Why not tonight?"

"Because I'm fucking tired right now."

She started to laugh, and clamped a hand over her mouth. He backed away from the lip of the roof, as if the dead might actually see his face floating over the edge like a big white balloon.

Janet peered out for a few moments and then motioned him closer again.

Together, they watched the shamblers. Once in a while, one of them shifted or moved forward, bumping into the fence, rattling the links.

"So, are you and Barbie married?"

"Angel," he said.

"Angel. Are you married?"

"No."

"Is she yours?"

"Yes."

"Well, if you want to keep her, watch out for the horn dogs downstairs."

"She's a big girl."

"And they're big boys."

"Thanks for the advice," he said firmly, ending that line of conversation. As they watched, another shambler stumbled along the side fence, rounded the corner and joined the others at the gate.

"It seems like they like to hang together."

"Good friends, great food," she joked.

"I'm told you stay up here all night watching over everyone."

"Yeah. So?"

"But you were awake during the day, too."

"Every day."

"So, when do you sleep?"

She pointed down at the shamblers. "Who can sleep with this shit going on?"

He shook his head. "You'd sleep better with bars on the windows."

Kevin rolled over onto his back and stretched. His body ached from sleeping on the floor, but he'd slept reasonably well. Angel sat on the desktop, staring out the small, ground-level window. He lay still for a moment, watching her from the side, her face lit by the tiny window. Her delicate neck and slightly upturned nose made for a lovely profile. A hundred and fifty years ago, they'd have captured her image in ivory on a cameo broach.

It was hard to reconcile that face with the career she'd chosen. Before the dead returned, she'd been the office manager of a small collection agency in Fort Collins. Kevin was a collections agent. The work was miserable. He hated calling debtors, he hated hearing the same excuses and promises and he hated being a hard ass to people in trouble. The problem was, entry-level positions in financial services were limited, even with his degree. He could be a bank teller. Or he could be the voice that made debtors curse their phones.

As the office manager, Angel was responsible for a certain rate of return on the debts they tried to collect. She couldn't afford to be understanding, or sympathetic or kind. But she could be just. And she was unerringly just.

Once, a woman returned Kevin's first contact call—a rarity—and explained in a calm, dignified voice that her husband had gone, taking their bank account with him, leaving her with the bills he hadn't paid in two months. She had two children and two jobs, and wanted to know what arrangements she could make. Kevin had no intention of playing hardball with the woman. She didn't offer the usual excuses or false promises. She was somebody with more than her share of trouble and heartache. He passed the case to Angel. She took the call without comment.

Later that day, she went to his desk. "Thank you for passing that woman on to me. That was the right thing to do." And so, when nothing better turned up in the job market, Kevin found that though he hated the work, he could tolerate the job.

And then, everything changed.

The world ended on a Friday. Kevin came to the collection office as always, despite the rumors of an epidemic. Most of the staff stayed home. Kevin's parents lived in another state. He called and reassured them. Then he went to work. His friends worked at the office. And he wanted to look in on Angel.

Broadcast news had finally begun to cover reports of overflowing hospitals and a military on the alert. For days, there had only been rumors, whispers on the Internet that were removed soon after they were posted. Stan, the assistant office manager, brought a television with him and placed it on an empty desk. No one manned the phones. They sat in a semi-circle, watching local news.

A traffic jam had developed outside. Kevin sat away from the others, watching the line of cars and the occasional fistfight between drivers.

Martial law had been declared in six states on the east coast, as well as California and Texas. The governor of Colorado scheduled a press conference for seven o'clock that evening, and then rescheduled for six. Meanwhile, the last-minute frenzy to buy food and supplies was on. Groceries and hardware stores were doing all of the business.

Stan spoke, his voice low and soothing, assuring everyone that things weren't as bleak as they seemed. It wasn't necessary. The staff was silent, numb with unanswered questions.

A television reporter warned of "graphic video footage," followed by a poorly focused clip of wounded, dazed civilians stumbling through a police line, mouths working. The action jumped from scene to scene, showing little or nothing at all.

"They could do better," Stan declared. He pressed in closer to the screen and shook his shaggy head. "This footage has been cut and censored."

"What is this supposed to show anyway?" one of the collectors asked. "It's stupid."

"Quiet, quiet," Stan said. "They're talking about the Center for Disease Control!"

"They ought to admit that there's a bio-contagion," the collector said. When he swallowed, his Adam's apple jerked. He was only twenty-five, but he'd already lost most of his hair. He patted the remaining strands on his forehead. "It's about time for a little honesty."

"Listen," Angel said. They were instantly quiet. The announcement was interrupted by a message from the governor. Martial law had been declared in Colorado. The clock showed just before five.

Stan sighed. "Well that's it." He turned off the television. "It's over." He slapped the counter top. The collector put his head down on the desk.

Outside, the sun slipped below the mountains, throwing a cold blue light across the streets and buildings. The icy sidewalks glistened in the dying light.

Angel closed her eyes and nodded, as if she knew they were waiting for her to speak.

"Stan's right," she said at last. "There's nothing left to do. Go home. Take care of your families."

No one moved. They'd suspected this moment would come, but

shock still etched their faces.

"Do you have somewhere to go?" one of the men asked. "Are you going to be all right?"

"I hope we're all going to be okay, Frank."

"I've enjoyed working for you," he said. "You were a good boss. I just wish . . ." He stopped. The words fell short.

She dismissed the other employees, one by one. Stan was the last through the door. "Come with me," he said. "The wife won't mind. We have a guest room."

Angel shook her head. "I'm fine. I'm going to stay here a while and lock up." She gave him a tiny wave. "You'd better go. I'm sure your wife is worried. Don't forget your television."

"Don't need it. Network news is depressing." He choked off a laugh, and then he was gone.

Now only Kevin remained, watching as she walked to the window. He could hear horns and a sound like a car backfiring in the distance. Then he heard her speak—a resigned sound, a deathbed sound. "That," she said, "is that."

She doesn't know I'm here, he thought. He cleared his throat. "It's peaceful in here now."

Angel jumped and whirled. At first, she didn't see him. He waved from the rear of the room.

"I didn't know anyone was still here," she said.

"I don't make a lot of noise. I didn't mean to scare you," he added.

"You should probably go."

He nodded and stood up. "Yes. We both should."

"I have things to do first."

"Like I said, it's peaceful now. But you can't stay here. The world has already turned. By tonight, there won't be a safe place left."

"They've declared martial law."

"Looters will outnumber the police a hundred to one. Any soldiers they call up are going to be sixty miles south, in Denver. Besides, kids in this town burn couches to celebrate football victories. They march downtown and smash windows. The police chase them off with teargas. How do you think they'll celebrate the end of the world?"

She shivered. "I don't know."

"I've been watching you."

"What's that supposed to mean?" Her face darkened, as if she'd realized for the first time that she was alone with him.

"It means I watched you dismiss everyone here. I think you planned to wait here until . . ." He didn't finish.

"What makes you think so?"

He said nothing.

"Don't you have anywhere to go?"

"I live alone. My folks are in Montana. I'll never make it there. The Interstates are one huge parking lot."

"What are you going to do?"

He measured his answer. "I'm going to look after you, boss."

Car horns blared again from the street below.

"No thanks," she said.

He shrugged. "If you decide to stay, I'll stay with you. If you decide to go, I'll tag along. You'll need me sooner or later."

She looked into his eyes. "Why do you want to do that?"

He blushed. "I like you, boss. Now that the world is collapsing, I might ask you out on a date."

A single laugh burst from her lips.

"You think I'm too young?"

"I think your timing is lousy."

He grimaced. "Speaking of timing, if we leave now, we'll get to a safe place. I live in an apartment building. The residents have already started to fortify the place. But if we wait much longer, we won't make it."

"So you think the stories are true?"

"Which story? They're all different." He stood and walked closer, stopping to stare out the nearest window. "I believe we're in danger. Tonight, the people on the streets will be looking for the last great party. Or they'll be looting."

"The police—"

"The police have families of their own. They'll stay home. Or they'll leave for home before long."

She stared at him for a long time. Finally, she pointed at the *computer on her desk and said, "I have to turn these off."*

"I'll help." Together, they shut down the office. She backed up her hard drive and locked the disc in the safe while he closed down the workstations.

As they were finishing, a loud sound jolted them both. "That's not a car backfiring."

She nodded.

"I'm a nice guy, Angel." He'd said her name as if whispering a prayer.

"I'm sure you are."

"Do you have family here?"

"No. My mom and dad passed away a few years ago."

"You need someone to look out for you."

Her gaze hardened again. "I don't need looking after."

"That's where you're wrong," he told her.

<hr />

Angel knew he was awake, still prone on the floor, relaxed as always, stretching like a puppy. Kevin could close his eyes and sleep each and every night, never moving—one long uninterrupted snore. She rubbed her sore eyes and tried to focus them on the fence across the yard. Five shamblers stood by the gate. She blinked a few times. The shapes blurred.

Angel knew that with another hour's sleep, her head wouldn't ache so much. She'd be strong enough to struggle through the day. But as each dawn approached, she found herself awake again, torturing herself with worry and guilt.

And the father of her baby lay on his back with a big grin for her, as if he were glad to see her.

"Shut up," she said.

He chuckled and stretched again. "I didn't say anything."

"Then don't start now." A half-smile crept up on her like a traitor. *He can make me smile any time he wants. It's infuriating!* She grabbed her shoe from the desktop and threw it at him. He blocked it, laughing, and she found herself laughing as well. That irritated her even more. It was just as well that they weren't working together today. She'd already had as much of him as she could stand.

After breakfast, Kevin went to Corey's basement room. "We've got to grab some equipment," Corey told him. "Janet is going to meet us at the door. She'll give us a weapon and ammunition in case something goes wrong. Here's the thing, though. We're only supposed to shoot as a last resort. Basically, we get to hold the gun. We can't use it. Unless it's an emergency."

Corey pulled what looked like a bazooka from the pile of debris in the corner. "Here. Take it."

"What the hell is this?" Kevin asked.

"It's a net gun. It fires a fifteen by fifteen foot net about thirty yards, covering up anything in the way. I don't use it for tagging, but it will come in handy if a crowd of zombies comes after us. At least, I think it will. It's meant to be fired from above, like from a helicopter."

Corey bent over, fiddling with a metal pole with loops at both ends. He held it out towards Kevin. "This is a catchpole. The loops are metal cable, covered in plastic. You drop this end over the zombie's head and pull the knob at the other end and the cable forms a noose. Then you hold on to these grips. This pole is five feet long. You get somebody by the head, and they won't be able to bite you or scratch you. Nifty, huh?"

"This stuff is pretty cool," Kevin admitted. "Where did you get it?"

"I told you, I'm a wildlife guy. I was working on my Masters. I studied wildlife corridors."

"I don't know what that means."

"There's a patchwork of natural habitats in Colorado, even with the cities and towns taking up so much open space. We looked into the effect of connecting habitats with natural corridors to allow the wildlife to wander between habitats. It's a way of coexisting with the natural world. You'd be surprised how quickly wild animals adapt to that kind of boundary. You get coyotes wandering in to eat some old lady's dog, of course, but you get that anyway in this state."

"How do the animals get along with the dead?"

Corey didn't miss a beat. "The deer and elk steer clear of them. Predators like zombies a lot. They don't run very fast. You're a smart ass, aren't you?"

"What exactly are we going to do today?"

"Well, we're going outside the fence to catch a few zombies. We'll tag them with those." He pointed to a plastic bag full of numbered metal tags. "I had some radio tags and a receiver in my pickup when the shit hit the fan. We set up the receiver equipment here in the lab, but as soon as I'd tag one of the bastards, he'd walk off north or south, up the highway, and within a day or two they'd be out of radio range. There's no way to follow up if they wander away, you know?"

"And all of this is to track their decomposition?"

"I'm telling you, the dead are rotting. And the more they ripen, the more they slow down. If I can prove it, we'll have an idea of how long it will take before we're all safe."

"How many have you tagged so far?"

"About fifty," Corey said. "I used to have a partner. Big Tom was really, really good at it."

"Where is he now?"

"He got too close." Corey tapped the rubber grips on the body of the catchpole. "Keep your hands on these. Don't go above the top grip, or you'll get bit."

"Do we need both poles?"

"No. Why?"

"I'd rather have this," Kevin said. He reached down and grabbed a crowbar.

"I've got a baseball bat. Aluminum. Would you rather have that?"

"This will do," Kevin said. "So what happened with Big Tom?"

"Like I said, they bit him and the wound got infected. I swear, the crazies in this place were almost glad. They had somebody to run tests on. Wanda nearly had an orgasm. She drained about half of Big

Tom's blood, looking for her damned parasite."

They headed up the stairs, equipment in hand. Corey kept talking, though his volume dropped noticeably as they reached the ground floor. "Wanda did a number on Big Tom. His skin went gray, he lost about fifteen pounds and his eyes sank all the way back in his head." He paused, looking back. "She took blood and skin, and just before he died, they took a freaking marrow sample from his hip."

"What happened then?"

Corey shrugged and looked away. Janet stood at the front door, waiting with the .32 in hand. She gave it to Corey, butt-first. "Don't fire this unless you have to."

"We know, Janet," Corey said, pushing past her, banging the catchpole off of the doorframe as he stepped outside. He glanced in both directions. Four shamblers still guarded the gate.

"What are they doing there?" Corey asked.

"Waiting for dinner," Janet answered.

Kevin followed them, the net gun and crowbar in his arms.

"How are we getting outside the fence?" Kevin asked.

"You and Corey walk over to the fence on the south side. That's the side facing the stadium."

"I know which way south is."

"Super. Once you draw a crowd, I'll give you the signal and I'll run over to unlock the gate. I'll have it open by the time you get there. We'll do the same thing when you come back."

"What do you mean?"

Corey sighed and pointed to the street. "When we get back, we go to the east side and make some noise. Then we circle around and go to the gate. Got it?"

"I guess so."

Corey handed the pistol to Kevin. "You're the gun guy. Don't shoot me by accident." He crossed the yard to the south end of the compound and began tapping the chain link to make noise.

"You don't tag their ears, do you?"

"No way. We tried that, but I had an ear come off in my hand while I was tagging, so I figured, fuck that."

"What do you do then?"

"The trick is to get them on their stomach, face down. I get them in a closed noose and pull, and they fall forward. That's my part of this. When they're down, you move in close and pin them. Then I tag their clothing. The shirt collar works nice."

"I pin them. You tag them."

"That's it. Don't worry. It's hard for them to reach up behind to scratch you if they're lying face down." He glanced at Kevin's jeans. "I'm glad your pants are in good shape. They could get you easy if you were in shorts."

"This seems pretty sketchy to me."

"It is. The most important thing you and I will do on the other side of the fence is to look for a zombie with an existing tag. That's what I want. If you spot a tag, you let me know."

"So we're going to wander around?"

"Pretty much. We'll keep our eyes open for supplies, of course. We might go into one or two apartments down the road."

"Sounds dangerous." Kevin tapped the chain link once. Two of the shamblers were already headed their way, drifting step-by-step around the perimeter. "Why don't you check out the cars?"

Corey snorted. "Most of them have zombies in them."

"Not in the trunks," Kevin said. "Not in the luggage racks."

Corey stepped back. "Say, that's a good idea." He slapped Kevin on the back. "That's a great idea. I guess it never occurred to me. The truth is, I hate getting close enough to stir them up. I keep thinking they're going to figure out how to use the door handles." He punched at the chain link again, making noise. "So how do we get into the car trunks?"

Kevin tapped the crowbar.

"Oh, I get it. Very nice."

"Now!" Janet called from across the yard.

The two men broke away from the fence, leaving the newly arrived dead behind them. Janet had the lock open at the west gate, as promised. They shot through the gate, Corey with the catchpole and tags and Kevin with the pistol, the net gun and the crowbar. They moved west, across the open field behind the facility, putting some distance between themselves and the fence.

A hundred yards in front, a dead woman in a red dress stumbled across the winter scrub, mud up around her ankles. She had no shoes, and her feet were badly decayed. "We go for her first," Corey said, pointing. "That red dress will be easy to spot when we go out again."

They slowed to a walk as they came closer. The woman didn't seem to notice them. Her vacant expression owed much to the empty eye sockets and the jagged hole where her nose should have been. Most of her teeth were gone. Her mouth had drawn inward, forming a tiny, wrinkled "o." When she sensed them, her lips pulled back in a grimace, exposing a single front tooth and brown, clotted gums.

"Now!" Corey moved quickly, dropping the loop over the woman's head and snapping the noose shut. He gave her a quick yank and she spilled forward, not reacting in time to catch her fall. Her head bounced once.

Kevin looked behind to gauge the distance between him and the three shamblers that followed. They were moving slowly but closing the gap. Kevin set the rest of his equipment down and stepped forward, putting his foot on the woman's back. She began to thrash, trying to reach back to his leg.

"Pin her flat," Corey said, holding the pole in place. "Keep her still."

Kevin bent close, close enough to smell the wet rot. He tried to pin her shoulder without touching her skin, but it couldn't be done. She was moving, and the sleeve of her dress was torn. Her skin felt oily and slick. The material had absorbed some of the corrupted flesh. The red cloth had turned brown with white spots. He shuddered.

"Hurry! Hold her head still!"

Kevin pressed the squirming woman into the mud. Corey tried to step around, a metal tag in his hand.

"Do it!" Kevin muttered.

"I'm trying!"

Corey struggled to avoid the woman's bite. Kevin groaned and held her face down with his hands. Mud and scabs stippled the top of her head. Corey knelt and put a tag on the woman's dress collar.

Kevin let go, still crouching. The shamblers were steps away.

"Shit!" He fumbled for the equipment, trying to pick it all up at once. Behind him, Corey unsnapped the catchpole loop and raced away.

Kevin kept fishing in the mud, finally coming up with the crowbar and pistol. He aimed the pistol at the lead shambler.

"No, not the pistol!"

Kevin scowled and switched hands, hoisting the crowbar. The first shambler came directly at him, scarred arms outstretched. Kevin swung down, driving through the dead man's skull, burying the crowbar three inches deep.

But when he pulled back, the crowbar stuck.

"Come on," Corey called, trotting away from Kevin and the shamblers.

Kevin jerked at the crowbar, trying to dislodge it from the dead man's skull. The thing stumbled forward, dropping to the muddy ground. It shuddered once and then lay still. Two other shamblers closed in. The woman in the red dress at his feet struggled to get back up, reaching for his leg and slipping back down in the mire.

"You could always run," Corey shouted from a distance.

Kevin swung the crowbar again—a glancing blow that dropped down and shattered the next shambler's shoulder with a crunch. The thing turned to grab him, but it slipped in the mud, dropping to its knees. It had been reaching for him with its good arm, broken, dirty nails missing Kevin's cheek by inches as it tumbled forward. The other shambler followed, tripping over the first. Kevin snatched the net gun and backed up, circling away.

"Are you okay?"

"I'm fine," Kevin muttered. "Thanks for the help."

"I have a pole. What did you want me to do? Pole them to death?"

"You could have used it to knock one down."

"You're the dumb ass that didn't run."

"If I lost the equipment . . ."

Corey set the pole end down and squared up. "Look. They don't want your equipment. They want you. You run away. Then you circle back and get the stuff. It's easy. You have a brain. They don't."

Kevin nodded and took a deep breath, his fear and anger subsiding. Behind them, the mud-covered shamblers struggled to their feet.

"You still have the gun, don't you?"

Kevin nodded.

"Good. Fucking Janet would have a cow if you lost that."

Kevin started to walk again. The shamblers were on the move, and he didn't want to go another round with them. Corey followed without speaking.

They traveled south towards Hugh's stadium, where Colorado State once played its home games. On the right, the foothills rose up like the rim of a massive stone bowl, cupping Horsetooth Reservoir. To the left, Overland Trail served as graveyard to five hundred cars and trucks. The open meadow between sloped downward to the south, a sluice box full of mud and dead weeds. Kevin slipped once, almost falling.

"That's another reason you don't fight them," Corey said. "This time, they slipped. Next time, you'll slip. Game over."

Kevin nodded.

After a while, Corey whispered, "Blind leading the blind."

Kevin shot him an angry look. "What's that supposed to mean?"

Corey tried to swallow a laugh.

"What's so funny?" Kevin stopped. The shamblers were thirty yards behind them.

"You wouldn't understand."

"Try me."

Corey rubbed his chin, as if to consider something. Then the crazy smile came back. "You know who Peter Bruegel the Elder was?"

Kevin frowned.

"He was a sixteenth century painter. One of his paintings was called, 'The Blind Leading the Blind.' It was a picture of . . ." He broke off, giggling.

"A picture of what?"

"Blind guys walking in a line, holding each other's walking sticks. In the painting, the lead guy goes down, and the others just keep moving forward, tripping on each other." He burst out laughing. "That's what those zombies looked like, coming after you."

Kevin tried not to laugh. "You're a fucking idiot."

"You were doing hand-to-hand combat with three of them, and I'm the idiot?"

Kevin turned and walked on so Corey couldn't see his grin.

<hr />

"I do the cooking," Trudy Kensington said with a slight lisp. "You can help by doing some of the cleaning. All of the main floors need to be vacuumed. The vacuum is in the maintenance room. The lab floors are tile, so they need to be mopped." She brushed her long, dark hair away from her eyes, sweeping it over her shoulders in a single wave. "There's a mop bucket and mop in the maintenance room. You can fill the bucket in the mop sink. It's in the maintenance room, too." She wore her yellow sundress like a uniform—shapeless, loose fitting, revealing nothing beyond her rank. The tiny tape player in the kitchen rocked an old Phish album loud enough to drown out some of her instructions.

"Do I clean the apartments downstairs, too?"

"Yes, but not until tomorrow. We only clean the bedrooms once a week."

"Where do I find soap for the mop bucket?"

"In the maintenance room. Haven't you been listening?"

"Sorry," Angel said.

"I'll be done with lunch by the time you're done cleaning. I have some greens, so we're having salad. And I have a few carrots left over, so I'm putting one in with the greens."

Angel paused and then said, "Sounds great." *Am I supposed to comment? I don't have a clue.*

"What sounds great?" Jason came in through the door under the stairway. He stood with his arms folded, taking in the room. He squinted and then smiled—a grand, beaming smile, as if someone had released a hundred balloons.

"Jason? Did you come to help scrub the counters?"

"I came to see how our new girl is doing."

Angel smiled. Trudy turned away. "Gosh, I'm not used to seeing you here in the kitchen."

"What do you mean?" Jason said, lowering his lashes. "I'm a cook from way back. My family came from New Orleans. Eating and cooking are Louisiana's state sports. I make a gumbo like nobody on the planet."

"I love gumbo," Angel said. "The hotter the better."

"Aw! That's my girl! I'm going to have to whip something up for you one of these nights, and see how you like it."

"I'd love that," Angel said. She turned to Trudy. "I'm going now."

"What do you have her doing, Trudy?"

Trudy turned, her hand on one hip. "Work. Don't you have any of your own?"

"Of course I do. But I'm an astronomer. I'm taking a break because it's the daytime."

"Great," Trudy said, turning away again. She had a small pile of greens in the sink. She stirred them gently, humming, as if she were alone.

"I'm headed off to clean floors," Angel said, waving.

Jason followed her. "I'll keep you company for a while," he offered.

"I'm not sure Trudy will appreciate that."

"Trudy doesn't approve of anything. You'll figure that out after a while." Jason crossed under the stairs to the maintenance room and watched while Angel filled the mop bucket.

"So, what does an astronomer do at this facility?" Angel asked, pouring a dash of degreaser from a jug into the mop bucket.

"That's a great question," Jason said, leaning back against the doorframe, arms crossed. He had a trim body with taut muscles. He took a deep breath and seemed to hold it in place at the top of his chest. "Just before the collapse, a comet passed by the earth. Astronomers named it 'Mort,' which is French for 'death.' Odd, don't you think?" He continued on without waiting for an answer. "It was the first, and probably the only time that particular comet passed our solar system. It came close enough to the sun on its way out to alter the comet's orbit, so it probably won't be back.

"At any rate," he continued, "the comet was odd for several reasons. First, it came damned close to Earth. Two hundred thousand miles! That sounds like a lot, but it isn't. In astronomer's terms, that's a near-collision. And, the tail was backwards. You know that comets have tails, don't you?"

"Yes."

"The tail of a comet is comprised of particles that spill out behind the comet as it moves. Actually, a comet has two tails. One is comprised of dust particles. The other is ionized gas. Out in space, the sun's radiation blows the dust particles the way wind blows a raindrop. That tail tends to curve along the path the comet came from. The other tail is formed when gases from the comet are ionized by the sun's magnetic field. An ion is an atom that has an electron knocked off, making it a charged particle."

"I know what an ion is," Angel said, plunging the mop into the bucket. The water turned the color of mud. Whoever used the mop the last time hadn't rinsed it. Angel made a mental note not to repeat the mistake.

"Anyway, the ion tail always points away from the sun. So if you looked at Mort, it looked like it was flying backwards. Crazy, huh?"

"What's that have to do with your project?"

"Well, Mort had an odd color. Green. Some scientists thought the color came from carbon and cyanogens, which are poisonous gasses. I didn't agree, though. I've been studying spectrographs of the comet. Do you know what spectrographs are?"

"Yes," Angel said, slipping work gloves on.

"Well, I think we're dealing with gasses that we can't classify yet. And the thing is, the comet's tail passed through the earth's atmosphere just before the zombie plague started."

"Which tail?" Angel asked.

"Exactly," Jason said, suddenly animated. He sloughed off his calm demeanor like a lizard shedding skin. His hands were suddenly uncontrollable, underlining his words with an ornate finger dance. His voice rose in pitch and volume, and his dark eyes lit up. "The ionized tail hit the earth's upper atmosphere. If I can figure out what the ions combined with, and what the resulting compound did, then I would have a chance to figure out how to undo this."

"Sounds more like chemistry than astronomy," Angel said, pushing the bucket past him into the hallway.

"Exactly! You understand exactly! That's wonderful!" He frowned suddenly, as if seeing her for the first time. "That's remarkable. Do you have a scientific background?"

"No." She paused. "I've got to work now."

"Aw!" he complained, adding, "You're right, of course." He watched her push the bucket for a moment, and asked, "You want some help with that?"

Angel shook her head. "No, you're very sweet, but this is my job." She headed into the hall, steering the bucket with the mop handle.

"Do you know why the comet was named Mort?" Jason asked.

"Why? Because they knew the dead would rise up?"

"No. It was an inside joke. Scientists are horny people. 'Mort' was short for 'la petite mort.' It's French for 'the little death.' You know, the moment after a really good orgasm. When you almost pass out."

"I've never heard of that," Angel said, frowning.

"That's a shame," Jason smiled.

<hr>

Kevin stopped and stared at the row of cars on Overland Trail. "Now what?"

"I heard a good idea about searching car trunks."

"Don't we need to tag more shamblers?"

"Nah. That last one was prime. First of all, she wore a red dress. She'll be easy to spot. Second, she's already back at the compound fence. She's just standing there like a cherry on an ice cream sundae. She's a great candidate for tracking."

"How do you document the changes? You didn't exactly have time to examine her."

Corey started across the muddy field, toward the road. "542223."

"Pardon?"

"I have to do my observations on the fly. I worked out a six-digit description. By the way, why don't you ever say the word 'zombie?'"

Kevin sighed. "It sounds so Hollywood. It's a cheap horror movie kind of word. It turns the whole Apocalypse into a comic book. This isn't a DVD. It's real."

Corey whistled. "Picky."

"Maybe. So what does the number mean?"

"Each digit describes some aspect of the subject. The first number rates mobility, one-to-five. The second number counts working limbs. If the zombie—sorry, shambler—is missing an arm, then they're a 3. Our girl was a 4."

"Interesting. How many zombies have you had a chance to reexamine after you number them?"

"One."

"One?" Kevin exclaimed. They stopped at the edge of the street, in front of the row of cars. "That's not very many, is it?"

"Nope. Like I said, they tend to wander away. So, are we going to pop some trunks?"

Kevin dropped his equipment, squatted and looked under the nearest car. Sometimes, the shamblers who couldn't walk kept crawling. He stood up and brushed his muddy hands on his jeans. "Okay. Let's give it a try."

"Give me the gun," Corey said.

"Why?"

"I'll cover you."

"Why? I'm opening a trunk."

"People did crazy shit when this whole thing started. I can imagine some family packing their dead grandma in the trunk, hoping to get her to a hospital or a shelter. That's not so far-fetched, is it?"

"Good point," Kevin said, handing over the pistol. He stepped around to the back of the car, a late-model Ford. When his knee bumped the rear of the trunk, a dead man inside the car sat up and lurched at the window, startling them both.

"Shit!" Corey shook his head and shoulders, pointing his gun hand off to the side. "Stupid old fucker." He gave a short, nervous laugh. Across the street, two shamblers headed their way. Both were severely decayed and moving slowly, step by tortured step. Kevin stared at them for a moment and then put the crowbar to the trunk.

It took him nearly thirty seconds to wrench the lid open. By then, the two shamblers were halfway across the street. The trunk was filled with clothing and photograph albums. A fishing pole and tackle box sat tucked on the right side. "Come on," Corey said, scooping up the net gun and catchpole. "It's time to move."

The two men headed north, back towards the compound. Kevin glanced to the mountains once and noticed that several shamblers were moving towards the football stadium. *I wonder if someone's holed up in there?*

After moving a block down the road, they stopped in front of a Subaru wagon with a storage shell on top. A woman sat motionless in the front seat. Blood smeared the passenger-side window. Kevin looked underneath the car, noted the nearest shamblers (including the two that made slow work of following them) and then climbed up on the hood. He popped the storage shell open and glanced inside.

"Anything?" Corey asked.

Kevin didn't answer right away. He pawed through some clothing and pulled a zippered pouch free. Medicine. "This could be useful," he said, tossing it to Corey.

"Say, this is a good find. There's some prescription stuff in here. I'm sure Coleman will know what they are."

"Who?"

"Rod Coleman—the old, balding guy. Pompous? He's the viral expert. Say, I wonder if there are any opiates in here?"

"This is something," Kevin said, pulling out a small box of ammunition. He popped the lid. "Twenty, no, twenty-five rounds. Now where's the gun?" He searched the rest of the shell, but found no weapon. Meanwhile, Corey took a closer look inside the car.

The woman still hadn't moved. He tapped the window and jumped back, flinching, but there was no movement. A shambler from the apartment houses across the street had begun moving their way. The two they'd already run from would join them in a minute.

"It doesn't make sense," Kevin said. "Bullets, but no gun." He hopped down from the hood, splashing mud in Corey's direction. Steadying himself, he looked into the passenger-side window, past the bloodstains. "Okay, now it makes sense."

"What?" Corey stood in a shooter's stance, gun trained on the approaching shambler.

"The gun is in her lap. She shot herself." He grabbed the door handle. Locked. "I'm going to open this up."

"You gotta hurry," Corey said.

Kevin wasted a moment trying to pry the door open with the crowbar. *Come on, come on!* He swung the crowbar and broke the window in. The woman inside was long dead. The smell was unmistakable. He started to reach in and stopped. There was a bloody hole on the underside of her chin. The top of her head was a scabby mess. *She shot herself in the head. She won't come back.*

"Got to go now," Corey warned.

Kevin reached in, fishing the gun from her lap. The smell nearly made him vomit, but he wanted the gun. *This is like sticking my hand in a sink disposal,* he thought, grabbing the gun by the handle. He backed away and looked up. The shambler was two steps away, arms outstretched. Corey fired, striking the thing in the temple, spraying brown matter and blood across the hood of the car.

Kevin jumped back, the gunshot ringing in his ears. "Holy shit!"

"That was fucking loud!" Corey said, relaxing.

"I thought you weren't supposed to fire?"

67

"We're bringing back another gun and some ammunition. Fucking Janet can spare us one bullet."

Kevin rubbed his ears. "Nice shot."

"You're welcome."

"Let's go now, okay?" Corey pointed back down the road. The two decayed, persistent shamblers had caught up to them again.

Kevin and Corey took off jogging, carrying the equipment, the medicine bag and the guns. Kevin rubbed his ear with his shoulder. The ringing hurt. He hoped there was some aspirin back at the compound. He could see the fence in the distance. Were there more shamblers than before? It seemed so. He hoped they wouldn't have trouble getting back inside.

Fifty yards down the road, Kevin stopped short, peering into a minivan. "This one," he said.

Corey stopped and shook his head at the car. "The windows are tinted. I don't like not being able to see in."

Kevin tapped the window. Nothing inside reacted to the sound. "It's a van. These things hold a lot of stuff. Maybe they packed some food."

"I'd rather stick to the cars we can look inside," Corey said.

"I agree," Kevin said. He stepped to the driver's side and smashed the wind wing with the crowbar. The smell of death and rot spooled out, and something inside began to rattle. Kevin nodded and stepped back. "Good call."

"I'm right about most things," Corey said.

Kevin walked on, spotting a white SUV on the far side of the road. "Let's try over there," he said. He dropped to the curb to look under cars. Then he made his way to the SUV and tried the door, but it was locked. Corey circled the mud-splattered vehicle and checked the driver's side. "Locked."

"Someone took the time to lock up," Kevin said, smashing the crowbar into the passenger's side window. The smell of spoiled meat stopped him. He looked carefully over the broken, pebbled glass, certain that the car was free of the living dead. Then he reached inside and popped the door.

The smell came from a cooler, stuffed full of rotten groceries.

"Damn it! What a waste!"

Corey stood close by. "What was this stuff?"

"Steaks," Kevin said in a sorrowful voice.

"Well, we've got company coming. Hurry up."

Kevin opened the back passenger side door and climbed in. After a few moments, he pulled up a small cardboard box. "Okay, let's go," he said.

"Good," Corey breathed. "I'm getting tired of close calls."

A block further down the road, they heard the bark of a dog. Corey set his load down in the mud and tried to call the animal over. "Part golden retriever," he said. "Look at that coat! Come here boy, come here." He took a tentative step toward the dog, but the animal would not be approached. It raced away, heading east, back into town.

"I haven't seen a lot of dogs," Kevin said.

"Yeah. I think dogs might be pretty good eating for these damned things. Come on. Let's move. I want to get back."

As they trotted off down the road, arms full, Corey took a good look at the fence around the research facility. "Am I going crazy? It looks like there are a whole lot more of them around the fence."

"You're right. There are more of them," Kevin puffed. "But you may still be crazy. So how do we signal Janet to get back in?"

"She's been watching us the whole time. From the roof." Corey was breathing hard, too. His trot turned into a run. The net gun, catchpole and crowbar rattled in his arms as he stumbled across the field. "There she is now."

Janet sprinted out of the back door and headed straight for the south-side fence, shouting and waving her arms. She slapped at the chain-link, drawing some of the dead away from the gate.

"This way," Corey said, racing to the southeast corner of the fence, drawing even more shamblers to the east, away from the gate. Kevin understood that he intended to circle the long way around the fence while Janet created a diversion at the south side. The lawn space between the east side fence and Overland Trail was narrow, but there were no shamblers at all—until they rounded the corner.

Two of the dead blocked the way. Corey swung around them in

an arc, but Kevin slipped in the mud, barely keeping his balance. They were on him by the time he regained his footing. One grabbed hold of his shirt, fingers too weak to hold the material when Kevin spun away. The other, a bald man in his thirties, snapped at him like a pit bull, broken teeth just missing his face. The shambler with the ruined mouth lurched forward again, but stopped, his head collapsing in a spray of blood and bone.

Corey pulled the crowbar from the bald man's head. The other shambler lay prone in the mud, pushed from behind. Kevin waited while his partner grabbed the equipment he'd dropped, and then ran for the back of the building. "Thank you," Kevin shouted. The words came out in a gasp. Sheer terror had sucked everything else from his lungs.

"Run," Corey shouted back, not pausing.

Turning the northwest corner of the fence, they could see the gate, untended by the dead. Across the yard, Janet ran back in their direction. No less than twenty of the shamblers had gathered where she'd been, fingers hooked into the chain link, pushing, mouths open and groaning. When she ran, they followed.

She reached the gate seconds before Kevin and Corey and began fumbling with the lock. "Hurry, or I'm going to waste your bullets," Corey threatened. The first shamblers rounded the southwest corner of the fence, just twenty yards away.

"Fuck!" Janet hissed, dropping the padlock key into the mud.

"Shit! Shit!" Corey dropped everything but the net gun. He waited until more of the shamblers had turned the corner and then fired. The gun went off with a lurch and a pop. The net began to expand immediately, catching on the chain link, twisting and bouncing harmlessly in front of the shamblers. Kevin set the box of groceries down, pulled the new pistol and assumed a firing stance. Fifteen feet.

"Get in!" Janet screamed, flinging the gate open.

"Get in!" Kevin echoed. Corey bent, grabbed his equipment and shoveled it inside the gate. He started in but came back for the groceries. Kevin fired point blank at the lead shambler, drilling a hole into the dead man's forehead. The shambler fell back, tripping the woman behind him. Another shambler reached out, touching Kevin's sleeve. He put the gun to her head and fired, knocking her back into the fence, spraying the chain link with red and brown.

"Get in now!" Janet screamed.

Kevin glanced around his feet, looking for equipment, and then slid through the gate. Corey slammed the door while Janet locked the padlock. The shamblers pushed against the gate, fingers through the links, mouths to the metal, their throats rattling.

"Fuck! Fuck!" Janet cried, stepping back, nearly tripping on the catchpole.

"We need to get inside," Corey said. "They're like goldfish. If we're out of sight, they'll forget us."

Janet nodded. Kevin grabbed the groceries and headed for the facility entrance. Corey followed, loaded with equipment. "I'm shaking like a rabbit in a stewpot," he muttered. The crowbar dropped from his arms, and Janet bent to grab it.

"It's okay," she said. "Get inside."

Bernard and Candice were there to greet them. They slipped into the lobby and shut the door. With the blinds pulled down, the horror seemed behind them.

"Oh my," Candice said, wringing her hands. "That was too close."

Kevin collapsed into a chair and began to tremble.

"Sorry about the gunfire, Janet," Corey said. "But we brought

72

back a new gun. What kind is it, Kevin?"

".38 special."

"And we have ammo," Corey said.

"No shit!" Janet said. "A lot of ammo?"

"No, but it's something." Corey seemed agitated. He couldn't stop moving. He settled into one spot, his feet together, locked in place, but his hands crawled over each other like spiders, dancing.

"We have food," Kevin said.

"That is so wonderful," Candice said. "You were very brave, and you brought back food." She paused. Kevin sat slumped in the chair. "You should be the one to take the food to Trudy. I know in my heart she'll be glad to see it."

Kevin tried to stand. His legs buckled. "Shit," he whispered, pushing himself up with his arms. He swayed for a moment and then stooped to grab the groceries.

"Are you all right, man?" Bernard asked.

"I'm not used to running."

Candice turned to Janet. "I'm sure you can see I was right," she said. Janet squinted.

"Where would they have been if you weren't there to let them in? They'd be dead now. You saved their lives by being here. You are in charge of security, and you guaranteed theirs."

Janet shrugged.

Candice gave her a wise nod, as if she'd made her point beyond debate.

As Kevin and Corey headed down the hall, Bernard stared at Corey's shoes. "Man, your shoes are fucked up. Look at all the mud." Corey flipped him off.

<hr />

In the kitchen, Kevin set the cardboard box on the counter. "What's this?" Trudy asked. She fingered the box's contents. "Pasta. Beans. Tomato sauce. Now that's a good one. We were out." She pulled up a small can and grimaced. "Anchovies? God, I hate anchovies."

73

She looked up. "Is that it?"

Kevin gave her a slow shrug.

"That's okay," she said. "You can go out again."

Corey peered through the open door. "Hey?"

"What?" Kevin asked, his voice slow and thick.

Corey held up the pack of prescriptions. "I'm giving this stuff to Coleman. You ought to come with me. You found the bag."

"What's in the bag?" Trudy asked.

"Drugs," Corey grinned.

"I want some!"

Corey put the zippered bag behind his back. "Nope. Coleman gets first shot."

"He needs drugs. Stiff old fart." Trudy turned back to the cardboard box of food. "If you're not going to share all the goodies, then you might as well leave."

Kevin left without a word, following Corey down the hall to the lab where Rod Coleman did his research.

The lab was a large, rectangular room, lit from above by banks of fluorescent lights. A row of tables lined each of the two long walls. Coleman sat at the far end of the right-hand row, working at a computer. The various workstations were divided by equipment and function. Kevin thought he recognized one of the devices. "Is this an autoclave?"

"Autoclave incubator colony counter," Coleman corrected. "One station down is an antibiotic zone reader."

The far end of the room was walled off, visible through three large windows. Corey pointed at it. "What's this?"

"An aseptic room. The university built it with a laminar flow system and U.V. lights to maintain test conditions." Coleman pushed the mouse away and pivoted on the chair, a frown creasing his bald forehead. "What can I do for you gentlemen? I'm working."

Corey held out the zippered bag. "We brought you drugs."

Coleman didn't rise from the chair, but his back stiffened and his eyes narrowed. "What have you got there?"

Corey came closer and handed over the bag.

Coleman unzipped it and dumped the contents out on the

counter, examining each container of pills one-by-one, offering a running commentary in a calm, dispassionate voice. "This one's a prescription antacid. Somebody had a reflux problem. And this one's an appetite suppressant. Somebody needed to eat smarter in more ways than one." He grabbed another bottle. "Okay, this is a little better. Doxycycline—it's a low grade antibiotic."

"Can it get you high?" Corey asked, an innocent look on his face.

"No, but it could cure your acne."

Corey slapped Kevin on the back and laughed. "Anything else?"

"Aspirins. That's good, actually. We're nearly out." He pulled at the bag, freeing one last bottle. The label brought a pained expression. He closed his eyes for a moment.

"What is it?"

"Sertraline. It's an antidepressant."

"Shit, we could have used a bigger bottle," Corey said.

Kevin looked around the lab again. "What do you do here?"

A look of hurried irritation returned to Coleman's face. "I'm looking for a viral source to the plague."

"Lots of empty seats in here."

"That's right," he said, as if someone had stated the obvious. "There are eight stations in this lab. Teams worked here."

"Why a virus?"

Coleman sat back on his stool and folded his arms. He stared at Kevin. "The way this disease spreads? A virus is the only thing that makes sense."

"But how would a virus bring someone back to life?"

"Tell him," Corey jumped in. "Viruses aren't really alive anyway, are they Professor? They multiply, but they're not alive."

Coleman waved him off. "It doesn't matter. I don't have the equipment or the manpower to do anything of value."

"There are other people in this facility," Kevin said. "Why aren't they helping you?"

Coleman snorted. "They have their own projects."

"I could help."

Coleman stared at him. "Well, you know what an autoclave is.

75

What do you know about microbiology?"

"Not a lot," Kevin admitted.

"Then you're in a little over your head, aren't you?"

Corey turned away, but Kevin wasn't ready to leave. "I can do grunt work."

"This isn't a field for grunts. Thank you anyway."

Kevin stood still. He looked into Coleman's pale blue eyes, and though he saw arrogance, anger and fear, he did not see duplicity. The man was telling the truth as he saw it. "There are other scientists here," Kevin said. "People who could help."

"Like I said, they have their own projects."

Kevin shook his head. "That's stupid. Tell me this—could they help you?"

"Probably not."

"You're a bundle of joy, Professor." Corey stood at the door, ready to leave.

Kevin started away and then stopped. "If it's so hopeless, why do you bother?"

Coleman scowled, his bald forehead creasing like corduroy. "What else do you do when the world ends? There's no television and there are no video games, so I do this. What would you have me do?"

Kevin pointed vaguely at the equipment. "I just wish there was a way to help you."

Coleman met his gaze, satisfied that he'd made his point. His frown softened, and his eyes seemed almost kind. "Let me get back to work, gentlemen."

Angel was cleaning and organizing the basement storage room when Kevin arrived. By the time she realized he was back, he'd gone to sleep on the carpet in their room, curled up in the corner. She left the light off and backed out slowly to let him sleep. *He was out there with those things. I hope he's all right.*

Later, she joined Trudy in the kitchen. "What now, boss?"

Trudy turned. "Your boyfriend found some food."

"Anything good?"

"No," Trudy said.

Angel waited. Trudy went back to cleaning counters.

"What did he bring?"

Trudy sighed. "Some pasta, some tomato sauce and some anchovies."

"You don't like anchovies?"

Trudy threw her washcloth down and put her hands on her hips. "You know their legs? Filaments! They're so fucking gross!"

"I don't like them either. So how much food?"

"For this bunch?" Trudy asked. "A couple of meals."

Angel smiled. "That's good, right?"

Trudy frowned. She had a pretty face, soured by a consistent frown. "No, it's not. We don't have a lot of food in storage. Those guys were supposed to bring me something to work with. Candice said so. She promised me."

Angel's expression went flat. "I'm sure they tried."

"I know that. But we're running out of food."

"How bad is it?"

"We have a dozen people here. Twelve! It takes a lot of stuff to feed that many people, you know? We're down to two meals a day, and Candice is ready to go down to one. Those guys only went out for an hour or two, you know? They should have brought back something. Are they going out again today?"

"I don't think so. Kevin's asleep."

"Asleep!" Trudy said, as if she'd learned that he could levitate. "Asleep! Jesus! If he's bored, he could do some cleaning, you know?"

"I think he's tired. I keep him awake at night."

"I don't want to hear about your sex life."

"No, not that. I don't sleep well."

Trudy glared. "None of us sleeps well, Angel. Not with those things out there. But you might notice—I'm not asleep in my room. I'm here making dinner for these brainiacs." She paused. "And you're cleaning floors."

Angel stood still.

Trudy turned back to the sink. She swabbed the faucet and fixtures with bleach water, glancing back once.

"What do you want me to do now?"

Trudy stopped. "Don't be pissy with me. I'm just telling you the truth." She stepped to the side and began swabbing the counters. "So, what do you think of Jason? You know, the guy who came to see you this morning?"

"I know who Jason is."

"I'll bet you do." Trudy fluttered her lashes, and Angel wondered if she was flirting. "So tell me—what do you think of him?"

"He's pretty," Angel said.

"Yeah he is. Even I think so." She came closer, brushing her long brown hair aside. "Do you like him?"

"He seems nice."

Trudy touched her arm. "Whatever. Do you like him?"

"I'm with Kevin."

Trudy gripped her forearm, her face intent. "Kevin doesn't own you, you know. I hate that shit. Men don't own women. No one can own anyone else."

Angel shrugged.

"I'm serious, Angel. No one can own anyone else. That's called slavery. What kind of hold does this guy have on you? Whatever it is, it doesn't matter here. You're free here."

Angel stepped back. "We're having a baby," she said. She hadn't intended to say so. She hadn't even told Kevin.

"Oh my God, you're pregnant?"

Angel nodded.

"Well that explains a lot. I wondered why you were with that guy."

"What's wrong with Kevin?" Angel's mouth turned down at the corners, and her lower lip betrayed her with a quiver. *They don't like him!*

"Nothing, nothing," Trudy said. She brushed Angel's curls from her eyes. "I didn't mean anything by it. I just meant that he seemed a little possessive, you know?"

"He's not a bad guy."

Trudy's expression turned melancholy. Her eyes glistened and closed. "They're all bad guys."

"Maybe," Angel said, trying not to argue. "But he tries."

"I'd like to agree with you. I wish I could like him. Tell me, what's so good about him?"

"He protects me."

Trudy slumped. "That's it?"

"He loves me."

"What's more important, the love or the protection?"

Angel shrugged.

Trudy turned back to the counter. She opened cupboards one at a time, looking inside and then shutting the doors. When she'd circled the sink area, she turned back. "You don't need him here. You're safe now."

Angel's eyes narrowed. "You're wrong," she said. "Let me tell you."

After they locked the office for the last time, she followed Kevin to his apartment. Electric power went down just after six, leaving the whole town in the dark. Their cars were useless—the streets were jammed—but Kevin stopped in the parking lot to retrieve two things from his trunk. The first was a flashlight. ("Don't ever lose the flashlight," he warned.) The other was a handgun. When she saw the gun, she frowned and gave a moment's thought to going off on her own, away from this coworker turned armed protector. Ten minutes in the streets made her thankful for the weapon.

They crept through the back streets, staying away from the main intersections, staying close to the buildings, tiptoeing through the shrubs. Shadows stumbled by, drawn by the headlights of abandoned cars. A cacophony of sound—horns, gunfire, screams, cries for help and the sound of breaking glass—crashed down on them in angry waves.

Overhead, the low cloud cover began to turn and shimmer, glowing with the reflection of a dozen fires. The acrid smell of smoke drifted on the cold night air, stinging her throat.

Kevin was silent. She tried to ask how much further they had to go, but he pressed a finger to her lips and shook his head. His eyes were wide and frightened.

Angel paced him, her arm touching his elbow. When he turned without notice, breaking contact, she pushed close, grabbing, her face pressed into his back or his chest.

His apartment was less than a mile from the office, but that safe haven seemed to telescope away as their progress slowed and finally stopped, halted by a woman's screams.

Headlights from trapped cars lit the lawn. A woman in a business dress stood shrieking at a group of men. Six of them surrounded her, laughing. Kevin and Angel stayed close to the perimeter of a building, hiding in the landscaping.

The men circled the woman, lurching forward and jumping back. Her blouse flapped open, material torn. She wore a light colored bra. She crossed her arms in front, covering herself, and the moment she did, one of the men jumped closer and tore at her skirt. She shrieked again. When she whirled to claw at her assailant, another man closed in and tore at her bra.

"We have to help her," Angel whispered.

Kevin pulled the hammer back on his pistol.

A passerby stopped at the curb. "Stop that!" he called out, his voice trembling. "Leave her alone!"

One of the men pointed a pistol and fired. The passerby leapt into the air and crumpled to the ground. At the sound of the shot, Angel slammed back against the cement wall behind her. "Oh my God," she whispered. "Oh my God! Where are the police?"

"There are no police."

One of the men grabbed the woman, locking her arms with a wrestler's hold. Another pulled her skirt down, leaving it around her ankles. Still another began to undo his trousers.

"Take that bra off."

"Look at that! Holy shit! Look at those!"

The men pushed the screaming woman to the ground, wrestling with the last of her clothing. The man with the gun shouted, "I go first!"

No one argued with him.

"Can you help her?" Angel asked.

Kevin shook his head. He looked into her eyes, his face as hard and unyielding as a cement slab. "I can protect you. Or I help her." He eased the hammer down on his pistol. "The rules of the world are breaking down now. I might be able to stop these men. Or I might not. And if they kill me, then you're next."

She glanced at the woman, motionless beneath the thrashing shape that had mounted her.

"We need to go. Follow me closely. If they spot us, you run. I'll catch up."

She nodded as if she understood, as if anyone could understand any of it. Later, when they were safe inside his apartment building, he took her to his room, pulled a second handgun from the closet and dropped it in her lap. "I'll be back," he promised. "I'm locking you in." The next thirty minutes were nearly unbearable.

When he returned—alone—he began talking about the plans he'd made. He told her about the supplies he'd gathered over the past three days. "I have a day pack and an overnight pack. I have some camping equipment. We have two guns between us. I have a little bit of ammo and lots of water. We can wait this out. People are going to survive this. It's not the end.

In the meantime," he explained, "the worst danger we'll face is the other survivors. People act badly when they're in groups. They become pack animals. Predators."

He talked about the future. He told her she was safe. But he did not talk about where he'd gone or mention the woman who'd been raped.

When she came to the room to check on him, Kevin pretended to be asleep. He lay on his side, facing the wall, his knees drawn up and his hands pinned between his thighs.

She didn't speak. After a few moments, she left, closing the door behind her. He pulled his hands free. They still shook.

He clamped his eyes shut and forced himself to breathe evenly. He could feel his heart race and stutter. *What the hell is wrong with me? God damn it!* He'd been just fine at the gate. He'd done what was needed. He'd found groceries and he'd added a gun to the facility arsenal. And then the bottom had dropped out.

"I need to rest," he thought.

Later, when his breathing slowed and his heart followed, he began to uncoil, and finally, to drift into sleep. Before he faded, a singular thought occurred to him. *This is how she feels. Every day. This is what it's like for her.*

I'm in her world now.

VIII

"Kevin? I need to talk to you." She reached out and shook him awake. The sun was down. He'd been asleep for a long while.

He rolled over, bumping into her. She sat next to him, her head down, blond curls falling forward to cover her face.

"What time is it?"

She shrugged. "I need to tell you something. I want you to hear it from me."

Kevin tried to sit up. His shoulders cramped and he fell back to the carpet for a moment, groaning and shaking his head.

"Are you all right?"

He tried to sit up again. "I'm cold." He propped himself against the wall and began to shiver.

Angel put a hand to his forehead. "You feel hot." Her voice dropped to a whisper. "You're burning up."

"I don't feel hot, believe me."

She sat back without speaking. Kevin sat, arms wrapped around his torso. She could see his silhouette in the dark, a black shadow shivering in a gray room. "Did they bite you?"

"What?"

"Were you bitten? Are you infected?"

He didn't answer. She thought she heard something like a mewing sound, but it may have been a laugh.

"Kevin?"

"No. No bites. No scratches."

"Do you have the flu?"

"I don't think so. I don't know." He sat up straighter. "Maybe so. I didn't think of that."

She let out a huge sigh. "Thank God."

He snorted. "Yeah, you gotta love the flu."

"That's not what I mean, Kevin. For a moment, I thought they'd bitten you." He didn't respond. "I couldn't survive that."

"You would do fine on your own."

"No I wouldn't. Why would you say such a thing?"

It was dark, but she could tell he'd shrugged.

"You're really not feeling well, are you?"

He shrugged again.

"This probably isn't a good time to talk, but there's something I have to tell you."

"Go ahead."

His voice was distant, as if he'd answered from the end of a hallway.

"You're scaring me," she said.

He cleared his throat. "I'm sorry. What is it you want to say?"

"I'm not sure how to tell you this."

"Let me help you," Kevin said. "Does it involve Jason?"

"Jason?"

"Jason Brock. The astronomer."

She let out an involuntary laugh. "No, of course not."

"He's been working on you pretty hard."

She laughed again and patted his arm. "You're jealous?" He didn't answer. "Well don't be. It's not very flattering."

"To whom?"

"To either one of us." She took a deep breath. "I think I'm pregnant."

His silhouette froze.

"Are you going to say something?"

"No."

Don't be angry with me, she thought. It took two of us.

At length, he stirred. "Well, I suppose it was inevitable."

"You probably should have bought condoms along with all the granola bars," she joked, her voice trembling.

"How long have you known?"

"Not long."

"Are you sure?"

"No, I'm not. They didn't lay in a store of EPTs here."

He sniffed. "I hope one of these folks knows something about babies."

"I worry about that."

"So. You said I might hear about it from someone else?"

"No, I never said that. But you might. I let it slip to Trudy."

"Why didn't you tell me earlier?"

"I don't know." *Because I thought you'd freak out.*

He sighed. "Hell, we're a couple of jerks, aren't we?"

"Are we?"

"Yes we are." His voice dropped to a whisper. "Can I tell you something?"

"Go on." She sounded calm. She wasn't. She was angry and hurt, and she wanted him to shut up.

"I didn't worry about a pregnancy. The truth is, I figured we'd be with the shamblers by now. I never thought we'd last this long. And I thought there was no harm in taking a little comfort from each other before . . ." His voice tailed off.

She felt the anger seep out of her, like air out of an old balloon, leaving only sorrow. "I know. When we left the apartment, I thought we were finished."

"So did I."

"Really? You seemed pretty sure of yourself."

He laughed weakly. "You're easy to fool."

She crawled over next to him and slid under his arm, nestling close. "We're supposed to go upstairs. They're having a meeting in a few minutes."

"They can wait," Kevin said. He was damp with sour sweat, still shivering.

"I heard you and Corey brought in some groceries," Angel said.

He stiffened. "Yeah, we found some things."

"Will you go out again tomorrow?"

"I suppose so." His voice was distant again.

"Was it bad?"

He didn't answer. Instead, he pulled her closer, pressing her face into his chest. "You're warm," he said.

<hr />

Candice silenced the group, not with words or the curt motion of her hands, but with a glance. Like a minister about to begin a sermon, her serene expression stilled them and replaced the whispers and laughter with quiet anticipation. She smiled but did not speak, waiting until just before anticipation took on an anxious edge. Then she nodded to Wanda, inviting her to begin. "Tell us what you've been working on."

Wanda swept her long, straight hair over one shoulder and took a deep breath. *Oh no! We're going to get the long version,* Angel thought.

Kevin sat stone-faced, leaning in so slightly that she almost didn't notice. "We're fresh meat," he whispered. She suppressed an overwhelming urge to laugh.

"Well! As you all know, I'm looking for a parasitic cause for the plague." She waited, glancing at Kevin and Angel, the two people who had not heard about her work. "Anyway, the problem is still the same—equipment and test subjects. It's very frustrating. I mean, I know that with some decent body imaging and a few fresh subjects,

I could locate the parasite and find out how to neutralize it."

Coleman turned away, visibly disinterested. Wanda gave him a quick, angry glance and then continued. "Since we have new members to our little family, I should explain a little about my research. Did you ever dissect a frog for high school biology?"

Angel realized that Wanda was waiting for an answer. "Of course."

"Your teacher probably hooked up a battery to the dead frog to show how the dead muscles would still contract with electricity, right?"

Angel nodded again.

"The dead can move," Wanda said, "but something living has to move them."

"Tell me. Do your parasites have batteries?" Coleman asked.

Wanda's kewpie doll mouth twisted into a scowl. She turned to face Angel directly. "This isn't unprecedented. Take Cymothoa exigua."

"Pardon?"

"It's a parasitic crustacean. It enters a fish's mouth through the gills and attaches itself to the tongue. It extracts blood until the tongue atrophies and drops off. Thereafter, the parasite acts as the fish's tongue by attaching its body to the muscles of the tongue stub. The parasite actually replaces an organ, without harming the fish. It becomes the fish's tongue."

"Tell me. Are the walking dead . . . fish?"

Wanda whirled to face Coleman. "What is your problem?"

"My problem is, you're wasting time—"

"I have a question." Kevin's voice was a stop sign, a red light. Angel looked over, surprised. Kevin's expression was serene, almost saintly. The calm in his eyes scared her.

"What is your question?" Candice asked.

"How is the parasite passed on? The reason I ask is, most of the population is affected, and I'm wondering how that happened. People avoided contact with the contaminated early on. I'm wondering how a parasite managed that kind of population penetration. It's almost like a virus."

"Oh, you've been talking to Coleman," Wanda said, as if she'd solved a mystery.

"Yes I have," Kevin said. "His lab is empty, and he needs some assistance. You clearly have a scientific background, and I'm wondering why you're not helping him with his project."

"I have my own project!"

"As I understand it, Rod's project is a long-shot at best. We'd improve our odds if he had some assistance."

Charles Broderick, the minister, interjected. "I'm not certain that we want to put all of our efforts into the same basket. From my point of view, both Wanda and Rod's projects are flawed because they approach the problem from a scientific point-of-view, rather than a more conventional, spiritual approach."

"You're an idiot," Kevin said.

Candice lurched, visibly shaken. "Excuse me . . ."

Kevin turned to Rod Coleman. "You need help with your research, right?" Coleman glanced at Candice, stricken, his lips pressed shut.

"Why is it that conventional science gets all the attention?" Todd Smith cried. "I'm every bit as much a scientist as these other professors. I have a Bachelor's degree in Cultural Studies, a Master's in—"

"It's the government," Bernard interrupted. "This outbreak is a result of government experimentation, and it may be planned. What's happening outside our fences is the result of genetically engineered—"

"The comet," Jason said. His voice was soft, but his words carried a cutting edge. "It's the only physical thing you can point to that might have caused the plague. The rest of this discussion is theoretical. Coleman? You're an expert in viruses, so of course, you think a virus caused this. Wanda? You're a microbiologist. And you think a parasite caused all of this? Surprise!" He slapped his forehead for emphasis.

Todd Smith gritted his teeth and shuddered. "All of this is just words. Zombies have been around for centuries. We need to go back to the original zombies and see what they were like and what they were in order to understand what we're facing."

"What are we facing?" Kevin asked.

"A concerted attack from some entity," Smith pronounced. "Zombies exist. They are documented—"

"We don't need documentation. They're outside, standing at our gates," Corey said. He looked angry, pale and disturbed.

"I think that's enough," Candice said. "More than enough. I'm asking you to each take a moment to breathe, a moment to calm down." She paused to demonstrate that order had been restored. "This is not who we are. This is not who we want to be. This is the way the world was, the reason the world collapsed. People who don't help each other, people who don't respect each other, always, always fail.

"If we stand together, we can't be defeated. If we stand apart, we crumble. It's as simple—and as just—as that. We deserve what we get. If we value each other as part of a family, we deserve the label 'human.' If we break down and call each other names, we deserve to join the dead."

Kevin blushed. He started to speak and then stopped. Candice wasn't finished.

"Let me ask you something. What sense is there in pooling our belongings if each of us clings to that last material conceit—our pride? Without Janet, you'd all be sandbagging your rooms and making weapons instead of looking for a cure. Without Trudy, you'd be cooking and cleaning up instead of doing research. Is she less valuable to our work than any one of you? Of course not!

And who would ration the food?" she continued. "Someone always wants to eat more than their share, just as someone always believes that their project is worth more than anyone else's. If left to your own devices, we'd be without any food at all. The point is, people, that everyone here is important. All of our projects are equally important."

Downcast faces turned away, unwilling to meet Candice's gaze, unwilling to look at each other.

"We're better than this." Charles Broderick's voice was low, bolstered by the resonance of a thousand Sunday sermons. "As the living world shrinks, those of us who are left carry the responsibility for mankind's end. How will we conduct ourselves? Will we finally embrace a God-centered way of life, or will we take the sins of mankind to the bitter end?"

"Amen," Trudy said. Her face pinched closed with contrition.

"Oh bullshit." Corey's words sent another shock wave through the room. "I'm not ready to join the zombies, and I don't think any of you are either. But we're not doing anything to better our situation! Instead of trying to survive, we're trying to play nice. What a circle jerk!"

"Corey!" Candice's face flushed with panic, splotches spread across her face from her neck to her hairline. "Why would you say that? What's come over you?" Something brittle in her cry brought silence to the room again.

Angel felt a familiar sense of dread creeping in, despite the fact that dawn was more than ten hours away.

Kevin cleared his throat. "There was this farmer who wanted his pig to win the grand prize at the county fair, so he stuck a cork in its ass and fed it a lot of slop." Corey let out a half-swallowed laugh. The others turned to stare. "Anyway, there was this monkey that got loose at the fair and . . ." He paused. "Ah, I don't remember this joke very well. The punch line is something like, 'The last thing I saw was that poor monkey trying to put the cork back in the pig.'" Silence. Kevin swallowed. "The reason I'm telling jokes is because I think I pulled the cork out of the pig here, and I want to try to put it back." He glanced at Candice, but she turned away.

"No offense, but it's too late," Wanda said, her bow-shaped lower lip quivering. "I have a good idea of what everyone here thinks of me. You can hide behind all the niceties, but it's all bullshit. Isn't it, Professor Coleman?"

"How about we talk about something important, instead of getting into a pissing contest?" Corey's face contorted with frustration and anger.

Jason turned, trying to calm him, his hands palm up and open. "Come on, guys. This is wrong. We don't need to do this."

"We're blowing it," Bernard wailed. "Blowing it!"

Trudy began to cry. Wanda scooted across the floor, wrapping her arms around her roommate. The circle broke into small groups full of gestures and conciliation. Coleman sat still, staring at Candice. She stared back, her eyes smoldering beneath her disheveled hair.

"This is unprecedented," she said at last, her voice still potent enough to command one last silence. "I think we need to get a good night's sleep. We will meet again tomorrow evening. Perhaps we'll all treat each other a little better tomorrow." She finished with a cold, angry tenor that lowered the heads of some. Corey scowled and looked away.

Candice stood arrow-straight, her feet together. She gave the room a final glance and headed down the hall. Kevin followed her. "Candice? Candice?" She didn't turn. He caught up to her, tapping her lightly on the shoulder. She whirled, her eyes wild and incredulous, her hair flying with the force of her turn. "Don't touch me!"

He stepped back. "I just wanted to apologize. I feel like I started something back there."

"The arrogance!"

"Pardon?"

"The arrogance! You come here uninvited. We take you in and share what little we have. And suddenly you know what everyone should do, what everyone should work on! And we should all follow your lead?"

"No, I never said that."

Candice pointed back at the others, her voice rising. "Everyone in that room heard you. Don't tell me what you did or didn't say."

Kevin backed up another step. "Look, I'm sorry if you took me that way. That isn't how I meant it."

Her face closed to him. She turned and walked off without another word.

"Kevin?" Angel stood ten feet behind, her hands folded.

Kevin watched as Candice walked down the stairs. He turned back, his face red and haggard. "These people are fucked. They're all fucking nuts." He tried to walk past Angel, but she grabbed his arm and held on.

"Kevin," she said. "They're in shock. They've lost everything. Everything!"

He shook his head and pulled away. "I need some air. I'm going up on the roof." His voice was gummy, as if his tongue had grown too

91

thick. He gazed at her for a moment, his eyes never locking on, drifting instead as if he were dozing off. Then he turned and walked away.

Angel watched as he went through the maintenance room door. *This place isn't a sanctuary!* she thought. *It's an asylum! These people are shattered. They're in pieces!* Then came a stunned realization—Kevin was in shock. He had all of the symptoms. Something had happened to him out beyond the fence. Or maybe nothing at all had happened. Maybe the cumulative pressure had taken its toll.

A thousand mornings flashed before her. The memory of a thousand suns turning her blood to ice. *They're all disturbed. And I'm the one with experience in dealing with depression. The only one.*

<hr />

He was alone on the roof for just a moment. Janet crossed over from the hatch and joined him at the west ledge. Below them, more than forty shamblers had gathered at the gate.

"There are so many," he whispered. Soft light from the lobby filtered through the blinds, lighting the shadows that stood at the chain link.

"It has me worried."

"Are we being too noisy?"

"Maybe. Bernard says the organs rot at different rates. The eyes go first."

"They do seem to respond to sound. On our way here, we spotted two kids who'd burned their eyes out looking at the sun. They didn't notice us until they heard us."

Janet snapped her fingers as if to test the theory. He stared at her in horror, backing away from the edge of the roof.

"Chill. They can't hear us if we whisper."

"What's drawing them, then?"

Janet shrugged. "Smell, maybe? Bernard says that smell goes last. What? What did I say?"

"Nothing." He stood scowling, his arms folded.

"Hey, don't be angry with me. I might be the only friend you have left in this place—except for that goof Corey and your girl."

"I didn't do anything wrong."

She tried to suppress a laugh. "Come on! Sure you did!" She continued in a lower voice, clearly meant to imitate him. "You're an idiot," she mimicked. "A stupid, fucking idiot."

"I didn't mean it like that."

She smirked. "Oh, you meant the good kind of idiot."

Kevin opened his mouth to argue, but there was no point. "You're right. I'm an asshole. But that minister is an idiot."

"I hear you," Janet said. "But do you think anyone cares?"

"They should care about finding an answer," Kevin said, pointing toward the fence below.

"No one's going to find a cure," Janet whispered. "In the meantime, we're doing well just to keep from killing each other. Half those poor bastards out there died at the hands of friends and family when the world broke down. Don't you know that?"

He turned away.

Janet stepped up to the ledge. "Candice is a freak show," she continued. "But no one at this facility is fighting and no one's trying to take charge. She makes sure of that. So they love her. She pisses them off, but they love her. You, on the other hand, scare them."

The sight of so many dead at the gate made him shudder. "The shamblers should scare them. Not me."

"The shamblers don't fight. They don't argue." Kevin could see her frown, even in the dark. She whispered a line from an old John Lennon song.

"Imagine?" he asked. "You know that song?"

"What, I can't know anything but hip-hop?"

"It's an old song, that's all," Kevin said. "But it's the right song for tonight." He pointed at the fence. "You're right. There's brotherhood for you." A sudden, helpless laughter took him. He backed away from the ledge, clamping a hand over his mouth.

She followed, her eyes white and open in the moonlight. She jammed a fist against her lips, as if to stem the fit of gallows humor.

"No greed!" he whispered through his fingers. "No religion! No nationalities!" His voice bordered on hysteria. "They're sharing the fucking world!"

They collapsed into a heap, arms wrapped around each other, laughter like screams. His stomach ached with release. He was able to control himself only when he felt the palm of her hand cup his face.

Her skin was soft, much softer than he'd expected.

"Oh God," she said, tears streaming from her eyes. "I thought I'd never laugh like that again." She groaned. "It hurts!"

He pulled away. "I don't think Candice would think it was funny," he said, evoking the only name that could reduce them to whispers again.

Janet sat back, her arms folded. She looked beautiful in the dim light, her face and upper body a study in sharp angles. Her ebony skin glowed in the moonlight.

"That's her utopia," he continued, trying to control his thoughts. "Mindless corpses, without any individual dreams or desires. We'll never be that unselfish."

She reached out to him. He pushed her hands away.

"I can't," he said.

She nodded and stood, brushing herself off. It took a long time. She was careful to brush every inch of her uniform pants. When she looked up, her eyes were dry.

"I didn't mention. Angel and I are having a baby."

Janet snorted. She walked back to the lip of the roof, shaking her head. He stayed back, unable to join her, unable to leave. He took a deep breath. The smell of rot was just a hint in the night air.

"You know what's sad?" she asked at last. "I might be the last one."

He started to ask what she meant. Then he thought about it and understood. "You're not. There will be other people."

"But I might be," she said. "The last black woman. How's that for alone?"

"You're not alone."

"Oh yes I am," she said, turning, her thin smirk back in place. "I'm alone in my room. And I'll be alone on the roof when you go back down to Barbie."

He started to correct her, but thought better of it. "There are plenty of people left alive. When this ends, we'll find them."

Janet looked down at the shamblers. "This is going to end, all right," she snapped. "But it's not going to end happy."

94

IX

Kevin couldn't sleep. He lay still, listening to Angel's soft snore. When he started to tremble again, he eased away, covered her with the blanket and crept to the door. He didn't want to wake her.

He decided to walk the halls of the facility. He supposed Janet was still on the roof, but the rest of them were in their rooms. The halls were empty. He'd been at the facility for more than a day, but hadn't had a chance to explore. When they'd first arrived, the place had seemed huge. Now, walking from the downstairs workstation to the lobby, he realized how compact the building was.

A single bulb over the stairwell provided the only light, casting its exhausted glow both upstairs and down. Kevin shuffled over the carpet, drifting like a ghost. The facility seemed devoid of human presence. He exhaled. It was a rasping, hollow sound.

The lobby was a stark vision of empty furniture and shadows. Kevin wavered for a moment, and then sat heavily in one of the chairs. He could feel his energy pour out, ebbing like the tide. *If I was in my room,* he thought, *I could sleep now. I could sleep forever.*

It was too dark to get a clear look at Kevin when they woke up. But when she heard his voice, she knew something was terribly wrong. Trudging up the stairs to breakfast, he moved slowly, as if he had no strength left. "You don't have to go out today," she said. "I really wish you wouldn't." He stopped and looked back. His red-rimmed eyes were cracked and ancient. He shook his head once and continued up to the dining room.

When they entered, all conversation stopped. Kevin stood, hands on his hips. "Good morning, everybody," he said with forced joviality. "How's everyone today?" A few mumbles answered him. Candice sat at the table, staring at the wall.

Janet sat in the corner, nibbling her breakfast. When it was clear that no one intended to say anything else, she did. "It's about time. I thought you were both going to sleep in."

Angel walked around Kevin, taking his arm as she passed, dragging him to the table. Trudy had made muffins from a mix—one muffin for each of them. Angel grabbed two and pushed one of them into Kevin's hands.

"Good morning!" Corey came in from behind them. He gave Kevin a playful shove. "What's up partner?"

A few faces registered quick, furtive smiles. When Corey reached for the muffin plate, Trudy slapped his hand.

"What?"

"Just one," Trudy said. "I know your tricks."

"I didn't take any! How can I be in trouble?"

"We're all on to your wicked ways, Corey," Wanda said. Trudy and Wanda began to laugh, and a few others joined in, seemingly relieved to have the tension broken. Candice stared at the wall.

"I hope you aren't allergic to blueberries," Trudy said to Angel as she took her first bite.

"No," Angel said, her mouth muffled on a muffin.

"I'm just kidding," Trudy said. "There's no real fruit in any of those mixes."

"Yeah, Corey. You should find us some fruit today." Todd picked at his Hawaiian shirt, looking for stray crumbs.

"You bet. My partner and I will find a big old berry farm and come back with a couple bushels. We'll make wine out of the leftovers."

"Good idea," Charles said. "That way, you could stay out of the communion wine."

Trudy and Wanda burst out laughing. "Reverend Charles! That's the first joke I've ever heard you tell." The Reverend blushed, but the corners of his mouth curved up in a furtive smile.

Corey grabbed a muffin and pulled Kevin to the door. "Come on partner! Let's get to work! Janet? Get off your ass and help us get out of the gate!"

Kevin glanced back as he went through the door. The others nodded or smiled, but Angel caught his stricken expression. *Don't go out there,* she thought. But she kept her mouth shut.

When Candice left, and Rod and Wanda headed to their laboratories, the conversation began in earnest. "Your boyfriend's a little closed-minded," Todd Smith said. He brushed muffin crumbs from his mustache and beard while he talked, spilling them into the open collar of his bright yellow shirt, where they became lodged in his graying chest hairs. "I've been studying the Caribbean for more than a decade, and I'm telling you, they have real zombies there."

"We have zombies here," Angel said.

"Yes, but which came first? It's an important question. The answers we seek here may have their roots in the islands."

"Let me tell you a little about zombification," he continued. "Voodoo priests supposedly had the power to reanimate the dead. The version you find in folklore is that these witch doctors would rob a grave of its recently deceased, animate the corpse and make it a slave. Cheap labor, after all, is a powerful motivator. Ask Walmart."

Angel gave him a tepid smile.

"Wade Davis was an anthropologist in the 1980s. He spent time in Haiti and Africa, tracing the roots of voodoo. He came across what he called zombie powder—a combination of ingredients that would transform a person into a zombie. The ingredients included a centipede, a certain kind of spider, one type of worm, several local plants, a few species of reptile and a puffer fish.

"It was the puffer fish that caught his attention." Todd leaned forward, his hands moving with the story. "One species of puffer fish—the fungu—is a notorious poisonous fish."

"People eat it in sushi," Trudy said.

"Not the poisonous parts," Todd laughed. "The fungu contains tetrodotoxin, a sodium channel blocker that shuts down the brain. Just a little can be lethal. But a small, controlled amount, taken through the skin pores by contact with a certain powder, leaves the victim paralyzed—catatonic."

"Why is that important?" Angel asked.

"Davis believed that voodoo priests used the powder prior to the victim's supposed death. Then the priest would bury the poor fellow. Much later, when the victim's mind was shattered, the priest would dig him up and release him. Of course, the victim was convinced he'd died and been revived. He would believe he was a zombie, and he would begin to act like one. Self-fulfilling prophecy, and all."

"That's amazing," Angel said. "But what about those zombies outside?"

Todd shrugged. "Well, there are several possibilities. When Davis had his powder analyzed by U.S. pharmaceutical labs, they found some TTX—the tetrodotoxin—in minute amounts. But that may or may not have been the powder's operating mechanism."

"You have to understand," Todd continued, "that the zombie tradition goes back all the way to Africa. There's some evidence that the consumption of brain matter by certain tribes may pass on hereditary diseases."

"So what are you saying? How are you using this information to help?"

Todd's pained smile was a warning. She had insulted him. He leaned back in his chair, regarding her through narrowed eyes. "I'm trying to reconstruct the formula for the original zombie powder. The components almost certainly include human tissues as well. It makes sense to me that the flesh and bone of one of these American zombies might make a powder even more potent than the original formula."

"What would you do with it?" Angel asked, horrified.

"If you can identify a toxin, you can identify an antidote."

"Oh, that makes sense. Are you a chemist, too?"

"Unfortunately, no."

Jason, who had been listening intently, knelt down next to Angel's chair. "I'm fighting the same problem. You remember when I told you about the comet's tail? I'd love to explore what chemical reactions occurred, but I'm not a chemist." He put a hand on her arm. When she started to pull away, he gave her a pat and withdrew his hand. "Your guy seems pretty interested in the science end of things."

"That's the problem," Reverend Charles said. "He's pinned all of his hopes on science, and none on spirituality." He pointed at Todd. "I, for one, would never doubt the possibility of Haitian zombies. There are too many phenomena that exceed the boundaries of science. I'm a theologian. I know better than to pretend I know everything."

"Tell him about your project," Trudy encouraged.

Reverend Charles was a sallow man, with dark, troubled eyes. He spoke in a soft, deep voice that promised comfort, but his eyes revoked the promise. "I'm searching the scripture for an answer."

"Tell her what you found."

"What's happening outside our fence was anticipated." Charles's lips were wet, and flecks of spit flew when he spoke.

Angel shivered.

"Zechariah 14:12," he began. "Their people will become like walking corpses, their flesh rotting away. Their eyes will shrivel in their sockets, and their tongues will decay in their mouths."

"That's from the Bible?" Angel asked, incredulous.

"That shouldn't surprise you," Todd said. "After all, Jesus was a zombie."

Reverend Charles turned angrily. "That's sacrilege!"

Todd held up his hands. "Sorry! But even you have to admit, the whole Lazarus thing sounds zombie-like."

The Reverend sat back, his voice full of sorrow. "There are other scriptures," he said, but he seemed to have run out of energy. He wiped his mouth with the back of his hand.

"Well I think it's amazing," Trudy said. "People don't believe in the Bible, but no matter what happens, the answers are there in black and white."

"Or red," Todd said. Trudy scowled at him, and he shrugged. "What? Jesus' sayings are in red. Don't be that way. I was agreeing with you."

"Let's not argue again," Jason said. "Maybe we should all get to work. A little hard work is all we need. Am I right?"

Trudy nodded and turned to Angel. "Okay, today is the day you clean rooms. Once a week, you go into everyone's room and tidy up. Don't be mad. I've been doing it for a long time."

"It's really helpful," Jason added. "It saves us time."

Angel stood. "I don't have a problem with that. Are the rooms unlocked?"

"All except for the room to the right of yours. You leave that one alone."

"Why?" The question was innocent, but the people around the table reacted as if they'd been accused. Trudy scowled. Todd looked away. The reverend wiped his open mouth again. Even Jason frowned.

"It's empty," Trudy explained. "Tell me when you're done. There's more work."

<hr />

Kevin hit the open gate running, the .32 in one hand and the crowbar in the other. Corey raced a single step ahead of him. Janet stayed at the gate; padlock in hand.

The two men ran without looking back, racing across the muddy field. When they'd gone a few hundred yards—surely enough to outrace the shamblers—they turned and stood staring, open-mouthed in shock and disbelief.

No one had followed. The shamblers stood at the fence, three deep.

"What the hell?" Kevin asked, his heart racing. He pointed with the crowbar. "They didn't follow us. They went back to the gate. Are they getting smart or something?"

"No way," Corey said. "Coleman says their brains are functioning, but at a much lower level. They see and they bite. They're like sharks. The filters that damper any primal action are gone."

"Filters?" Kevin asked. "Primal action?"

"Sorry," Corey said. "Remember? Wildlife was my field of expertise."

"What's holding them there?"

Corey shrugged. "Maybe they sense food."

Kevin stepped back. Corey stood in front of him with his hands on his hips, staring at the facility fence. "So, Coleman says they still function a little? Their senses, I mean?" No answer. "Maybe even the rotted ones might be able to smell?"

"Makes sense."

"They bite, but they don't eat, right?"

Corey shrugged. "I don't know. No one knows. Coleman doesn't know any more than the rest of us, though he thinks he does. Maybe they don't eat. Maybe they just bite."

"Wonder what they're smelling?"

Corey laughed. "Not Trudy's cooking, that's for sure." He laughed again. "And we don't have any little kids. You know, like human veal."

Color drained from Kevin's face. "Angel's pregnant."

Corey turned and looked at him, his face open with laughter until he saw Kevin's expression. The grin froze on his face. "You're shitting me."

"No."

Corey frowned. "Don't tell anyone."

"Some people already know."

"Does Candice know?" He shook his head angrily. "It doesn't matter. She will eventually. Just don't say anything. The longer it goes on, the harder it will be for her to do anything to you."

"Why? What would she do?" Kevin knew, of course. *The bitch will put us out.*

"I don't know, man. Just don't say anything."

They began to walk south, toward the football stadium. "Do you think the shamblers are smelling Angel?"

"How do I know?" Corey asked. He kicked at the mud beneath his feet, sending a wet clod flying in front. "They did start gathering after you two arrived."

"Shut up. There could be other reasons." Kevin moved off to the east, toward the line of cars on Overland Trail. Corey followed without speaking.

Kevin chose a small blue Volkswagen first. Nearly two months in the open air left a coat of silt on the paint. A glance through the window showed him that the car was empty. He tried the door, and then unlocked it with the crowbar.

Corey stood behind him, watching for shamblers. One old woman was heading toward them, step by halting step. They had plenty of time. "Anything?"

"Clothing," Kevin said. "More clothing than any six people could use."

"We don't need clothing."

"No shit." Kevin moved on to the next car, a Subaru Legacy. Again, no one inside. He popped the trunk with the crowbar and jumped back. The trunk was empty.

"Try the door."

Kevin glanced up. The old woman had started into the street. He turned back to the door, jamming the bar into the crack behind the handle. It took him nearly thirty seconds. The old woman was at the car, circling from the far side. Corey stood in a firing stance with his own pistol.

Kevin waved Corey off. He set his pistol on the passenger side seat and moved in to meet the woman, swinging the crowbar at her head. When the bar hit, the woman's head cracked open, spilling the insides like egg salad. She shuddered once and then dropped to the concrete.

"You're one cold son-of-a-bitch," Corey said, lowering the gun. There was admiration in his voice.

Kevin held out the crowbar. Pus dripped from the tip.

"More coming, ice man." Two more shamblers stepped into the street.

Kevin ducked into the car and began sorting through boxes. Then he began to laugh.

"What? What's the matter?"

Kevin pulled a brown box the size of a microwave oven from the back seat. He tore open the top and held it out. "Granola. A case of it." He laughed again, an unsteady sound, part irony and part despair. "So now I'm back to granola."

"That's fucking great," Corey said, grabbing the case. "There must be twenty boxes in here. That's food for days. What else is in there?"

Kevin pointed at the shamblers, halfway across the street. "Watch them. I'm climbing in." He slid into the front seat and climbed over into the back.

"Hurry up, God damn it!"

"Shoot them if you have to," Kevin said. "There's more stuff back here." He pulled up another box. "This is a case of those meals. You know? Add water and heat? They taste like cardboard, but they last forever."

Corey fired his pistol, cursed, and fired again. "I need some help!"

"Let your breath out before you shoot," Kevin said, pushing the box toward the open door.

"Hurry up!"

Kevin pushed the box out and climbed into the front seat. Corey hollered and fired again. The shambler that had been reaching for him jerked away, blown back by the shot. It toppled to the ground. The other shambler lay in a heap at the Subaru's rear tire.

"Nice," Kevin said.

"Fuck!" Corey said. "You're supposed to help me!"

"You did great on your own," Kevin said. "But the shots are drawing a crowd." He stepped from the car and picked up the second case. "You carry the granola. Let's head back to the compound. This is all we can carry anyway."

Corey picked up the granola. "You're too fucking happy right now."

"I feel great!" Kevin said. "Fuck these things. They can't hurt us!" It felt true. Adrenaline surged through him. The weak feeling was gone. It had been an aberration, a fluke. He was fine now. They headed north, back to the compound, and Kevin began to run.

"Janet's on the roof," Corey said. "You can see her up there, watching us."

"Good. She can get us through the gate."

Corey stumbled, nearly dropping the box. "I can't see my feet, carrying this box."

"You know what we ought to do?" Kevin asked. "We ought to circle the fence and pitch these boxes up over. That way we won't be stumbling around when we make a run for the gate."

"Now that's a good idea." Corey exhaled, blowing vapor. "It's fucking cold out here."

Kevin laughed as they approached the fence. The shamblers had gathered to the west at the gate, standing three deep. There was a stretch of fifty feet at the east side of the fence that was unguarded. "There!" he said. "Hurry! Let's ditch these boxes!"

Corey ran up and pitched the granola. It hit the barbed wire that topped the fence and dropped back. Kevin's case went over on the first try.

"You suck," Kevin laughed. He pointed his gun at the fence corner, where shamblers had begun to make their way toward them.

"My case is heavier," Cory growled. He bent to retrieve the box. He had only seconds to heave the case. It struck the top wire, turned over and dropped to the other side.

"Yes!" Kevin shouted. "Come on!"

They ran to the street and turned. Janet wasn't on the roof—surely she was on the far side of the grounds, ready to open the gate. They circled to the north, easily avoiding the shamblers that had come to meet them. They waited until there were too many to count and then they began to run, circling to the north and then the west. Janet was at the south side of the fence, rattling the chain link, trying to draw still more away from the gate.

"We're going to have to shoot our way in," Corey called.

Kevin waved his crowbar and gun, shouting.

Janet saw them and broke for the gate. Two shamblers waited at the west fence. "Shoot them, shoot them," she screamed. Kevin rounded the corner and headed straight for the shamblers, nearly pin-wheeling with the effort. Corey slipped in the mud and landed on his tailbone, losing his gun.

Kevin reached the first shambler while Janet fumbled with the lock. He crushed the shambler's head with his crowbar. When he tried to pull the crowbar loose, it stuck fast, yanking the shambler back and forth like a puppet. No, not again! The other shambler grabbed Kevin's shirt, pulling close to bite. Kevin pushed the .32 under its chin and fired, blowing hair and bone up through the skullcap, spraying bits into the air—a fine mist that hung like a brown fog.

Janet popped the lock and swung the door open. Kevin stepped inside and turned. Corey was crawling toward him, fifteen feet away.

"What are you doing?" Kevin screamed.

"I'm hurt!" Corey said. A half-dozen shamblers converged on him, arms outstretched. "Help!"

Kevin started back through the gate, but Janet grabbed his arm and pulled back violently. "No!" Kevin wrenched loose, spinning and falling with the effort. When he looked up, the shamblers swarmed over Corey, biting and pulling at him. Kevin heard the gate door slam and saw Janet snap the lock shut. Shamblers lunged at the gate, rasping and tugging at the chain link.

Janet pulled Kevin to his feet and ran him toward the door. Corey's screams stopped him. He turned back, knocking Janet into the mud. He raised his hand and found the .32 still in it. He cocked the hammer and fired at the shambler that sat on top of Corey, biting the back of his head. The shot punched into the thing's temple and blew out the side, taking the right half of its face off with the bullet's exit. The shambler fell forward, blanketing Corey. But there were others, snapping and scratching at him. Corey let out a squeal that rose to an incredibly high pitch and then stopped. Kevin fired again and again, but the pile of shamblers writhed above Corey's corpse, unstoppable and insatiable.

Janet grabbed his arm again, dragging him back to the facility entrance. He let himself be pulled along. The euphoria he'd felt was gone, replaced by a dull, throbbing horror. He felt his legs go first—a trembling that left him unable to stand. Then his hands began to shake. He dropped the gun. It hit the linoleum of the lobby. *I'm inside!* He dropped to the floor. From the corner of his eye, he could see Bernard staring through the blinds.

"My God!" he said. "They're eating him! They're actually eating him!"

Kevin tried to sit up, but his legs spilled out in front of him, and he dropped back, slamming his head against the floor.

Angel stood in front of the locked door, wondering what was inside. She had a good idea. *This place is poison,* she thought. *Kevin was right.* She reached out, fingers splayed open, stopping just short of the door. *If I had a key, I'd open this room now.*

Everyone else in the facility knew the answer to this little mystery. *I'm not blind. I saw their faces. Everyone's in on the secret,* she thought. *Everyone knows but Kevin and me.* Despite the talk about "family," they were still outsiders. They'd given up their things. They'd gone to work. But there was an unspoken period of probation, a character test they may have already failed.

She turned away from the door to find Jason sitting at the computer station at the center of the room, one elbow on the table.

"You scared me," she said.

"What are you doing?" The boyish grin was gone, though he did not seem angry.

"Cleaning rooms."

"Mine too?"

"Yes."

He stood up. "Would you mind getting to mine now? I like to be there when the room is cleaned. You understand, don't you?" He went to his door, the center room on the west side, and opened it up for her. "It's not too bad in there," he promised.

Angel stepped into the room. It was a small office with a desk and bookshelf, bare except for a half-dozen astronomy texts. The original contents of the room had been stacked in the corner behind the door, including books, picture frames, files and papers, topped by a telephone, cord torn from the wall, the handset smashed into two pieces.

He followed her gaze to the telephone. "There was no one to call," he explained. "I got tired of looking at it." His voice was low, much lower than usual. He leaned against the wall, still staring at her. "Do you know how beautiful you are?"

Angel stopped and turned. "Jason, you're a very nice young man. But I have a partner."

"Partner!" The smile returned, but with a sardonic turn to the upper lip. "I like the way you put things. You have a way with words."

"Thanks." She looked around the room. It was dark, like her room. The sun wouldn't angle around to this side of the building until later in the afternoon. "With everything piled up in the corner, there isn't much for me to do in here. I can vacuum."

"Sounds good."

She went out into the main room to retrieve the vacuum cleaner. When she returned, he sat on his empty desk, legs dangling.

Jason's face was draped in shadows, making his stubble seem darker. "I hope you don't mind some friendly advice."

She plugged the vacuum in without answering.

"Your guy is on everybody's shit list."

"Why is that?"

"Well Candice thinks he's trying to take over. And she's not the only one. Janet said he was pissy about handing over your supplies."

"That's not fair," Angel said. "He handed over everything. He just wasn't expecting a commune."

"None of us were, but when Candice started talking about living the right way and setting an example, it sounded pretty good. I mean, everyone generally agrees with the principles we live by here. No right-minded person disagrees. We share things, and we care for each other's needs. What's wrong with that?"

"Nothing, I suppose."

"What's Kevin's problem, then?"

"He doesn't have a problem."

"Well, I guess you have to support him. But you must admit that this is a pretty great setup. We're all doing our own thing, pursuing the work we were trained to do; the work we were born to do."

"Yes. Me too." She switched on the vacuum and began to push it back and forth across the carpet.

"That isn't what I meant," he said, shouting over the whine of the machine. "I meant we're each doing our own thing, without any competition. There's no wasted effort."

"Yes. Well, lucky for you there weren't two astronomers here." Angel moved the vacuum around the desk, behind Jason. He turned back, looking over his shoulder, following Angel's quick, expert movements.

When she crossed to the front of the desk, he hopped off to get out of her way. He waited until she was done to speak again.

"I'm off on the wrong foot with you, aren't I?"

"Not at all," Angel said, unplugging the cord and wrapping it on the vacuum's side brackets.

"That's good, because we could be friends."

"I'm sure we will be."

"And I know you have some kind of thing going with Kevin, but if that doesn't work out for you, I'm letting you know I'm interested."

She pushed the vacuum toward the door. "All done."

"And unless I miss my guess, you're interested, too. Just a little."

She stopped. "I don't want to mislead you."

"Oh, don't worry about that. Besides, you might just like a change." He stepped closer. "I'm a nice guy, Angel."

"I'm sure you are—" He cut her words off with a kiss.

She pushed him away. "Don't do that again."

"You'd like it if you let yourself."

"I'm with Kevin."

"He doesn't own you."

"Yes. Yes he does. And I'm one possession we're not going to share." She started out into the hall, and then turned, her face stricken with cold fury. "And don't do that again."

"What? Kiss you?"

"No, not that. I don't want you to talk about sharing and caring and use it as an excuse to take what you want."

"Aw, you're angry. I'm sorry."

She turned away. That was when the screaming began.

||||||||||||||||||||||||||||||||

Kevin pushed his way up, past Angel's arms, past Janet who knelt at his feet. Shoving Bernard aside, he struggled to the window. He pulled the cord, raising the blinds, opening a view to the west fence, where dozens of shamblers pushed at the fence. Corey's body lay still, just ten feet from the gate.

Corey. His friend.

One of the dead knelt by Corey's corpse. The shambler had been a man, middle-aged. He wore dirty, pale blue boxers and one dress shoe. Gaping holes in his torso revealed gray ribs and an empty chest cavity. His neck had been torn open as well. A flap of skin dangled below his ear.

The shambler was eating, pulling chunks of Corey loose and shoving them in his mouth. He made a show of chewing. Bits of skin drenched in blood dripped down his chin and onto his ribcage. After each bite, the shambler used his fingers to tamp the food down his throat, making room for another mouthful. The food stayed in his neck, creating a bulge, pushing against the tear. Bite after bite the bulge grew, swelling like a tumor, finally ripping the flap open, spilling bits of Corey out onto the lawn.

"It's fucking looking at us!" Bernard wailed. The kneeling

110

shambler did seem to be looking at the window.

"That's enough!" Candice had arrived. She strode to the window and began to lower the blinds.

"No!" Kevin shouted, grabbing the blind cord, pulling it out of her hands. "Everybody needs to look out the window."

She stumbled back as if she'd been struck. "Have you lost your mind?"

"They need to see."

"Who are you to tell these people what they need to do? Are you a dictator? Do you own this facility?" She stepped forward again, grabbing for the cord. He pulled it aside, out of her grasp. She bumped into him, crying out. "What, are you going to hit me now?"

Kevin turned, his round face dark and drawn. "Where were you all when we needed help getting back in? Why weren't you at the fence, helping Janet? We needed decoys! Where were you?" He clenched his fists.

Candice stepped back, realizing he might indeed hit her. "You're a thug! A common thug! Janet!"

Janet stepped between them, pushing Candice away. Kevin tied off the cord, yanking the string in a tight knot. "Why are you doing that?" Candice demanded.

Angel stood behind Kevin, her hand on his back. "Please! His friend just died."

"They don't give a shit about Corey," Kevin said.

"Don't you say that! Don't you dare say that! You have no right to say that to me!" Candice pushed past Janet, thrusting a finger in Kevin's face. "Corey was my friend! You've known him for two days!"

"Control yourself," Kevin said. "You're spitting."

"Oh! Oh!" She covered her mouth with her hands, stunned. Then her face changed, her features flushed blood red. As she started forward again, Janet grabbed her from behind, pulling her away.

Kevin watched as Janet took her from the room. At the back wall, Rod Coleman stood with his eyes closed. Wanda and Trudy huddled together, weeping.

"Take a look," Kevin said. "That's our reality. Or do you want me to close the blinds?"

"Yes," Bernard said. Tears ran down his cheeks, leaving streaks. He pulled up the flap of his tee shirt and dabbed at his eyes. "Please. Shut the window."

Kevin turned to the girls. Wanda nodded. Trudy turned away, refusing to look at him.

"If you want it shut, shut it yourself," Kevin told Bernard. He walked down the hallway to the stairs, past Coleman, past the girls. Jason stood by the railing, shaking his head.

Angel followed, unable to look at any of them.

They sat in a circle. Only Candice had the nerve to meet a gaze, to lock eyes without blinking. Her expression was stern and stiff, promising judgement.

"Angel is a nice girl," Trudy said. "She's been a great help with the chores."

"She's a great gal," Jason said.

"Angel's not the problem," Wanda said. "Kevin is. I'm not afraid to say it. That's what we're talking about, isn't it?"

"We're talking about whatever you think we should talk about," Candice said. "If you believe that Kevin is a problem, then who am I to question it?"

"I don't think he's a problem," Janet said. "He's done good work since he's been here. What happened to Corey wasn't his fault. I was there."

"Actually, Janet, aren't you the one who complained about him when he first got here?" Candice's cheeks flushed just a little. She brushed back a wisp of gray hair.

"He's cocky. That's not a crime."

"I don't know," Trudy said. "He's pretty obnoxious."

"Come on. If being obnoxious was a punishable offense, we'd have thrown Bernard to the zombies a month ago." Janet's attempt at humor failed. Bernard looked shocked, and the others looked disgusted.

"Okay, you appear to have some special reason for defending

him," Wanda said, her lips pursed. "But we're talking about whether or not to let him stay."

"What special reason?"

"Is he a danger? Will he ruin what we're doing here?"

"I asked, what special reason? I want an answer."

"Well God, Janet!" Wanda said. "It's pretty obvious that you two have some kind of thing going. He spends every night with you up on the roof."

"Fuck you, Wanda."

"No, fuck you Janet. You think I'm afraid of you because you carry a gun? Not here, not in this facility!"

Todd Smith interrupted. "We're doing it again. We're arguing over minor details instead of talking about the issues."

"And what are the issues?"

"I'll tell you what isn't the issue," Todd said. "I don't give a rat's ass who wants to screw whom. What I care about is whether this guy is messing up our chemistry. We had a good thing going here. Now, everybody's in an uproar. This is all about keeping our work going so we can find the answer to the plague."

"That's a very important point, Todd—"

"He's not messing with you," Janet said, interrupting Candice. "He's been an advocate for your research, hasn't he Rod?"

Coleman looked up. His complexion had paled to the color of ash. His wet, unfocused eyes would not meet Janet's gaze. "Candice is the reason we're able to work here. She set us free to pursue what we do best. Anything disruptive hurts us all."

"Coleman! The man supported your work!"

"Disruptions are bad. Period."

"What happens when you're the disruption? What happens when you're the bad guy?" The room fell silent, as if Janet had crossed an unseen line. The others stared at each other, startled. She held her breath. Frightened, docile faces floated before her, and it chilled her to her soul.

"What do you mean?" Candice asked.

"I mean," Janet said, scrambling for words, a look of panic in her eyes, "we all can be a pain in the ass sometimes. I don't want to think that if I have a bad day, it will end up with me outside the fence."

"Janet! How could you think such a thing? We would never put you out!" Wanda's voice was sincere.

Candice was silent.

"Janet!" Jason said. "What you do here is important. You protect us. You're our defense."

Janet glanced at the closed window blinds. "I still need help."

"I have something to say." Bernard's face twisted as he spoke. "I don't need someone telling me I have to watch my friend get eaten. I don't need that. I don't appreciate that. It was bullshit."

"Yeah, what was the whole Corey thing about?" Trudy asked.

"Corey was his friend," Jason said, looking down at his feet. They were all silent for a moment.

"We can't send someone out beyond the fence alone," Reverend Charles said. "That would be a sin."

"The sin," Candice said, "is repeating the same mistakes, over and over, instead of casting them out."

Reverend Charles stared at Candice, his dull gaze narrowed. He took a deep breath and then whispered, "You're a hateful woman."

Everyone began to shout at once. "What are you saying?"

"Reverend Charles!"

"No! You're wrong!"

The circle broke apart. People spun off into private arguments, gesturing and waving their arms. Candice stood, moving from a lotus position into a perfect, tall stance, arms outstretched, a look of pained love on her face. "People," she called. She had more than enough weight with the group to command their silence again. "This is perhaps the most important thing we've ever considered. Let's not vote without thinking first."

She looked to the reverend before continuing. "We have to be fair and just. Sleep on this tonight. Consider every aspect. Then vote with your heart. We'll meet again tomorrow. Tonight, meditate on this. Pray, if that is what you do. Then decide the right thing to do. We'll vote. We are a democracy here. I know you'll do what needs to be done."

"I didn't think I'd see you up here tonight." Janet stood on the roof. She spoke without turning.

"I wanted another look at Corey," Kevin said. He walked to the edge and looked down at the pile of bones and cloth that had been his friend.

"He didn't reanimate," Janet said.

"They opened up his head. Nothing left to come back."

The sky was cloudy and dark. No stars. Kevin could barely see Janet. The glow through the first-floor blinds was enough to light the yard to the edge of the fence. That was all. The shamblers at the gate were black silhouettes.

"They seem to get along well," Kevin said.

"Yeah. I read something once about how condoms collect in the ocean. When they get flushed out to sea, they end up gathering on coral reefs. Thousands of spent condoms, clumped together. It's an accident. Or a miracle."

"Charming. So, are they kicking us out?"

"Don't know yet. Your friend is welcome. But they seem to want you gone."

"Why?" The question was part plea, part anguish. "I did everything they asked."

"You don't believe in the dream," Janet said. "And this dream needs believers. It punishes non-believers."

"Maybe you're right." He snorted. "I can't believe that twelve people won't get together under life-threatening circumstances."

"It depends on your philosophy," Janet said. "You think people are smart. You think they can argue and agree to disagree and all that shit. Candice doesn't. She can't risk debate. People might decide to do what she believes is wrong. Period."

"Did you guys have some kind of meeting?"

"Yes."

"And what did you decide?"

"Candice said we should sleep on it."

Kevin nodded. Below, the dead numbered in the hundreds. The ones nearest the fence bounced against the chain link, making it sing like a Vegas slot machine, the tinkling music of chaos and empty promises. "A condom jamboree, huh? Damn. That's as good an explanation as any."

Janet stared at the fence. "Like our own personal coral reef."

"I'm not talking about the shamblers. I'm talking about the brain-dead fuckers downstairs. I want my gun back. I want my backpacks."

Her answer came slow and low, like a whisper of regret. "You gave them up in good faith."

Kevin turned to Janet, grasping her elbows. "Janet! You know that gun is mine. The Ruger? It's mine! I can do without the backpacks. They belong to us, but fuck it! I need the Ruger. I can live without the rest."

"Calm down. Let's wait and see what they say."

Kevin stepped away from the roof's edge, as if stepping away from the edge of sanity, afraid that he'd shout and stir up the creatures below. Couldn't Janet see what was at stake? Would they really put him out without arms, without a means of defense?"

"Come on, Janet. It's a minimal request. Give me the Ruger and you can keep the .32. Give me the Ruger and the ammo box. Give us a fighting chance."

Janet stood still in the dark.

"What the hell? Is this a death sentence? What about Angel? Do they intend to execute us both? Why? I didn't do anything! Do you think I did anything wrong?"

"You pissed Candice off."

"Is that a capital offense?"

Janet turned. Her face was a dark cameo. "Like I said, let's wait until tomorrow and see what they say."

Kevin looked down at the shamblers bouncing against the fence. "If they decide to push on those posts, we're all dead."

"I know it."

"Tell me something. You're smart. You know something about security. What's happening here is stupid. Stupid! There's no attention to defense. How did this happen?"

"I was a security cop," Janet whispered. The cloud cover broke for a moment, lighting her face. She was dark and beautiful, all angles and

116

sadness. "I worked around campus. When the plague hit, my supervisor told me to start carrying a weapon and live ammunition. I did. I was at the lab just down the way, when one of the lab techs got bitten in the throat. There was a lot of blood. I think the dead woman caught him in the jugular. Anyway, he reanimated right away. He started biting, and we ran like hell. I came over here, thinking I could use the phone. I just wanted a telephone. That's what happened. And now, here I am.

"We listened to the radio, and followed the Internet. The rioting started right away, and it just didn't seem safe to go home. Within a day, zombies showed up at the fence, and so we all stayed. I kept thinking police would come, or maybe soldiers.

"I know you don't like Candice," Janet continued. "But she saved us. We were at each other's throats those first few days. Bernard showed up after the television stations went down. We almost didn't let him in. Candice went out to the gate herself.

"She knew we needed to do something, to work at something. She put us to work, made us feel important, like it was okay to hope. It was like having your mom there to tell you the right thing, to scold you if you started to feel sorry for yourself.

"Some of these people worked in this building," she continued. "Trudy worked as a janitor for the university, and Jason worked on campus. They all came together under Candice.

"She's a scientist, too, you know. An entomologist. She studies bugs. This was her lab, really. They studied pine beetles here. Hell, I'm surprised she didn't come up with an insect theory for the plague."

Kevin snorted. "She was too busy running her little community."

Janet sighed. "She did good things for us, Kevin. We were lucky she was here."

"Then why does she scare you?"

"I'm an outsider. I'm black. I do what I'm told, so everyone's nice. They smile and everything. But if I fuck up, I'll be out there with the dead."

"Why do you think so?" Kevin asked, his voice dripping with sarcasm. "They sure don't think of themselves that way."

"Of course they don't! They think they're doing the right thing! They have all the answers. They aren't wasting time thinking about themselves; they're on a mission. They're going to save the world, and in the meantime, they're going to right every single motherfucking wrong ever committed by mankind! That kind of utopian shit requires full cooperation. God help anyone who gets in the way!"

Kevin kicked the ledge and walked away.

"It gets worse," she added.

Kevin walked back, trying to control his emotions. "What?"

"We're unarmed."

"What?"

"We're unarmed. We don't have any ammo."

"What are you saying?"

"I'm saying we're defenseless."

"Wait a minute! You said, when I brought in my guns, you gave me shit. You said 'Is this all?' as if I was a dumb ass for bringing in so little ammunition."

"I hoped you had more."

"How much ammo do you have? How many guns?"

There were no Venetian blinds to pull down to make the question go away.

"Four guns. Three now; Corey's gun is outside the fence."

Kevin stood still, trying to breathe. "How many rounds?"

"Less than seventy."

"There's a hundred shamblers down there," Kevin said, pointing. "How are seventy rounds going to do us any good?"

Janet didn't answer.

"Fuck. This place is a death trap."

"What do you want me to do?" she asked.

"We have to drop whatever bullshit projects we're working on and make a weapons run. We need guns, ammo, swords, baseball bats—anything! And every person in this place needs to be a part of the defense."

"Even if you could find more weapons, they won't listen to you. They don't believe in defending themselves. They don't believe in violence. It's part of the old world."

"Do they believe in being eaten alive?"

She shrank in the thin moonlight. "They believe in Candice."

"Wake up!" Kevin shouted, pounding on the doors in the basement. "Wake up! We need to talk now!" Janet stood at the foot of the stairs, a tired, resigned expression on her face. She pulled at her hair with one hand, twisting it around her finger, tighter and tighter, until it hurt. She kept the other hand on the butt of her pistol.

Angel was the first one out the door. Kevin's face was speckled with red. His eyes were shock white. His mouth pulled taut, thin-lipped with anger.

One by one, the others came out. Bernard came stumbling from his room in a tee shirt, trying to pull his pants on. "What's wrong? Are they inside? What happened?"

Jason was one of the last to emerge. He peered out before fully opening the door. Encouraged by the sight of others, he stepped out into the main room.

"What's happening?" Candice came fully dressed, but her puffy face and reddened eyes made it seem as if she'd been asleep.

"I'm calling a meeting," Kevin said.

"That's not your place!" Candice said. "Your fate will be decided tomorrow. In the meantime, you won't help your cause by—"

"This isn't about me. It's about all of you." A moment of silence from Candice was all he needed. "You have three guns and about seventy rounds of ammo. That's it. That's all you have."

Candice scowled, sending deep wrinkles and creases through her face. "Many of them already know!"

"What is he saying?" Trudy asked. She stood in a nightshirt, arm in arm with Wanda.

"It's just more bullshit," Wanda said.

"Seventy rounds," Kevin repeated.

"So?"

"There's a hundred or more of those things outside the fence. Seventy rounds won't stop them."

"Outside the fence, you say? Oh my! They're outside the fence!" Candice's voice ended in a raspy shout.

"Janet?" Kevin turned back to the corner near the stairs. "If they decide to push, can they take down the fence? Yes or no?"

"Yes."

"And what will make those mindless things decide to work together? Who will direct them? They need functioning brains in order to follow direction."

Kevin laughed. It was an ugly sound, part frustration and part loathing. "They're pretty good at acting in concert. And I can tell you one thing—if they can do something, they'll eventually get around to it."

Candice crossed her arms in front of her chest. "What's your solution?"

"We need a weapons run. Janet, myself, and one other person should go to town and hit the gun shop on College Avenue, the sporting goods places and Jax Army Surplus. Maybe some of the flea markets, too. We hit them all. We take guns, ammo and swords."

"Baseball bats," Janet added.

"Anything we can use. And when we get back, everybody in this damned place goes out on the grounds and stands on the east side fence to draw the shamblers away from the gate—the way you should have done for Corey."

"And how many weapons will you leave us here? And who will fire them?" Candice wore a grim look of triumph. The others nodded in agreement with the unstated point.

"Are you seriously saying the reason we can't go to get weapons is because we don't have enough weapons?"

"That seems completely evident," Candice said. "And it's all hypothetical anyway. You act as if you had a place here."

"People, the fence is good, but it's not enough!" Kevin turned his back on Candice. He would not sway her. He had to address the others. "If you get trapped on the roof, you'll die. You can starve or dehydrate, or you can let the shamblers take you."

"Janet addressed that concern last night," Candice said, stepping around him. "We put food and bottled water on the roof, just in case."

Kevin turned to Janet, confused.

"You had a good point about being trapped up there," Janet said.

Kevin slapped his forehead with the palm of his hand. "What's that going to do except prolong your death?" He turned to Jason and Rod. "Come on, guys! We need weapons. And everyone needs to be ready to use them!"

"I think the fence is a pretty good defense," Rod said.

"Maybe we could block the basement windows," Reverend Charles said. "I've worried about those windows."

"Absolutely," Kevin said. "And we need to reinforce the ground floor windows, too. If the shamblers can take down a fence, they can break plate glass. We need to do all those things. But we also need weapons."

"This is not how we address issues here!" Candice stepped in front of Kevin again, blocking him. She gestured wildly with her arms, and he moved back to avoid looking as if he were crowding the old woman. "We bring these issues up at the meetings! We stay with the rules we have in place! We don't change them at a whim!"

"This is an emergency," Kevin said.

"There's always an emergency! The terrorists are coming! Code orange! The zombies are going to work together as a team!"

"Coleman!" Kevin said, backing away. "The shamblers can sense us. That means they have some frontal lobe capacity. Doesn't it?"

Coleman shrugged.

"Come on, Professor. Do they have frontal lobe activity or not?"

"The question is complex. I don't think you have enough grounding in neurobiology to understand the answer."

"Try me."

Coleman's face went blank, thin lips pressed together, the corners of his mouth turned down. His eyes narrowed as if he were considering his answer. "If the frontal lobe is functioning properly," he said at last, "the impulsive actions of the amygdala are balanced by the anterior cingulated cortex. Because that balance is missing, there is no restraint on impulses like biting and scratching. And, their lack of coordination indicates damage to the basal ganglia. Does that answer your question?"

"Is the damage instantaneous, or gradual?" Kevin asked.

"What is the point of all this shit?" Trudy wailed. She turned to Angel. "Can't you shut him up?"

Kevin felt his stomach drop. He was losing. And Angel's life hung in the balance! "Coleman, they can move their limbs. They can walk. Their bodies are still working on some level, aren't they?"

"Corpses grow hair and nails after death," Bernard offered.

Coleman shook his head. "No, that's a myth. The scalp and the skin around the fingernails shrinks, so it looks like hair and nails are still growing." He looked at Kevin. "But I agree that the ambulatory corpses must have some body processes going on."

Angel spoke up. "On our way here, Kevin and I saw a pile of brown stuff that smelled unbelievably bad. I didn't say anything, but when I saw it, I thought it was . . . poop. Zombie poop. Is that possible?"

Coleman shrugged, helpless. "I suppose so. The body processes slow to a crawl, and there is definitely necrosis in play. But we're talking about nature. If the body is moving, then fuel and oxygen have to be processed."

"I'm not sure that's so," Todd Smith interjected. "There may well be a spiritual component that you're not considering."

Coleman waved him off. "I'm not discounting the spiritual perspective. But I'm talking about nature. And in the natural world, there's no free lunch. You can't get something for nothing."

A glance at Candice told Kevin that she was about to interrupt. He rushed on. "So if the dead are fresh, do the processes work better? Specifically, do the brains work better?"

"It's possible." Coleman's frown deepened.

"So a fresh corpse could lead, and the older dead might follow?"

"That's ridiculous," Candice said.

"Why is it ridiculous?"

Coleman waved Kevin off. "You're trying to ascribe conscious behavior to those things. But the fact that there's frontal lobe activity doesn't mean they can think. On some level, they know we're here. They want in. That's all. There's no thought to it."

"Okay, forget it," Kevin said, his face gone slack. "But I'm still talking survival here. What's wrong with wanting to shore up our defenses?" His voice took on a pleading tone. He held his hands out in front, palms up.

"Janet is in charge of our defenses, not you."

"Janet? Tell her! Tell Candice you need help."

"I need guns and hardware." Her voice was a cold whisper. "I need help."

"Of course we'll help you, dear." Candice seemed to relax. She stepped to the side, blocking Kevin again. "I am so sorry you all had your night's rest disturbed. I feel personally responsible . . ."

Kevin turned to Janet. "She's nuts. I want my guns and packs."

" . . . and I hope you will all try to put this out of your minds."

"Now, Janet! No more bullshit. I need the guns and packs."

Candice whirled and screamed. "They're not yours! They're ours!"

"They're mine, bought and paid for. Janet?"

"You are not going to touch that equipment," Candice said. "If you are ready to leave us, then gather your things—"

"You have my things."

"THEY'RE NOT YOUR THINGS!" She shouted into his face, her nose just inches from his chin. He leaned back, trying not to bump her.

"This is way out of control," Bernard said.

Jason agreed. "There's no reason for you to leave. I'm against it. Angel is pregnant. She shouldn't be traveling."

"Pregnant?" Candice backed up a step, confused.

"Wanda says that's why the zombies are lining up out there. They can smell her baby." Wanda hissed at Trudy to be quiet, but the damage was done.

"It's not right to put them out," Jason repeated.

"Pregnant?" Is that true?" Bernard seemed mystified.

Todd Smith slapped his leg and stood up. "That's it, of course. That's it! The damned things never came around until these two arrived. If they leave, the zombies will leave."

"You didn't tell us you were pregnant," Candice said. Her eyes narrowed to small, puffy slits. Her folded hands, her perfect posture and her frown were a condemnation, as if Angel had committed some great betrayal. "You should have said something."

"How could it possibly matter?" Angel whispered, near tears.

"Pregnant women have their own special odor," Todd said.

"That's absurd," Jason said. "None of us have had a hot shower in weeks, and you think they can smell a baby? Come on!"

"I'll leave," Kevin said. "But Angel's going to stay. You're not putting her out."

"That's not your choice," Candice said. "It's the group's choice."

Angel held up one hand, silencing the room. She stood still for a moment, eyes closed, tears brimming. Then she walked over to Kevin, grabbed his hand and took him to the door of their room and pulled him inside.

Kevin sat down on the carpet, facing the wall. "Wake me when it's dawn," he said. "I know you'll be awake."

"I'm certain I will be," she answered.

Outside the door, the discussion continued.

The sun crawled up again, and Angel was at the window to watch. The first rays lit the rows of shamblers. The ones in front bounced against the chain link, forced forward by the ones in back. She tried to count them—an exercise in fear and frustration. There were at least a hundred at the back fence. A closer look revealed more on the sides.

Can they smell me? Can they smell the baby? Do they prefer infant flesh? If they could smell her, the shamblers would follow her wherever she went. There would be no escape.

"This is the day we die," she whispered.

Her hands drifted to her belly. She caressed the area with both palms, a soft hello. Boy or girl? She'd always wanted a girl. She used to visit a small, upscale clothing shop in Old Town Fort Collins, browsing through small knit outfits, tiny dresses and soft, pastel blankets. When one of the girls at the office had a baby shower, Angel went to the shop and spent a fortune on gifts, dreaming of the day when the baby would be her own.

Kevin groaned in his sleep.

The deepest sorrow of her life settled in to stay. "I'm so sorry," she whispered, tears running down her cheeks. A thousand memories that would never be fluttered away like game birds at the sound of a shotgun. She sobbed.

Kevin stirred and rolled over. "Sun up yet?" he asked. His voice was full of gravel.

"Yes." She tried to say more, but couldn't speak.

"Did you sleep any?"

Angel shook her head no.

"That's okay." He sat up, brushed his clothing and looked at her. There was something in his gaze that frightened her. "I'm going to say goodbye now," he told her.

She slumped, leaning against the wall next to the window. She'd expected this turn. "I'm going with you."

"The hell you are. The fence might hold. And when I'm outside, I'm going to see what I can do about luring some of those damned things away from here. Don't argue with me. Once I'm gone, the pressure will be off. These people will leave you alone."

"Bullshit," Angel said without turning from the window. "You said this place was a death trap and the people were crazy."

"If I take you outside, we'll both die. If I have to go, I'll do what I can to make things better."

Angel stood up. "Grab the blanket. It's something. Maybe Trudy will give us some food."

"I don't need it," Kevin said without explaining. "And I'm telling you to stay. That's an order."

She looked at him wearily. "I'm yours. That's how it is. You gave me protection. Now I'm giving you a baby."

"Some trade."

She tried to smile. "I don't think anyone can actually love anyone in this world. Not now. But I care for you. And I'm going with you. I'm ready for whatever happens."

He wiped his mouth. "I can't protect you anymore. I'm breaking down." His voice wavered. Something inside of him collapsed, and he finished in a rush to get the words out. "The thought of going out there again makes me want to piss myself. I'm no good for this now. I can't save you. I can't save the baby."

"I know." She tried to touch his arm, but he pulled away.

"You don't get it," he growled. "I can't protect you. The deal is off."

"And you don't get it. I don't care. I don't want to bring up a child in this world. I don't want to think about everything that could go wrong to end our lives. And I don't want to fit in with people who are living in a coma, stumbling from day to day without thought or purpose. I'm not talking about the ones outside the gate, Kevin. I mean the people in here!"

He seemed to want to hold her, to comfort her. He reached out, a tentative gesture that died and dropped away, arms dangling at his

126

sides. He slumped, his head down, unable to meet her gaze. He'd lost weight in the past few weeks, as if he'd been whittled down to a stick. His arms had been muscled once. Now he was pasty and limp, a man headed for a nervous breakdown. How had it happened? Angel shivered. *And what does he see when he looks at me? Has the same thing happened to me?*

Kevin launched himself at her, wrapping his arms around her. He whispered, "I love you. It means nothing now, but it's true. I love you. It's all I have."

She nodded, in tears.

He pulled away. "Now, fucking stay here." He opened the door.

Janet was there waiting.

She held the Ruger and a box of ammo. "Whatever you plan to do," she said, "you'll need these."

He took the gun and ammo, stopping to search her face. "Why are you doing this?"

Janet stepped back and extended an arm. Jason, Reverend Charles and Bernard sat at the workstation in the center of the room. "Six votes, counting you and Angel. They can't kick you out."

Kevin stared, his mouth slack.

Angel grabbed his arm. "You're staying!"

"Why am I getting the gun back?"

"It's your fucking gun," Janet said. "This shit won't come up again if you carry a gun."

Kevin inclined his head. "Thank you."

"We need to lock this place down," Bernard said. Fear wracked his face, turning a half-smile into a rictus.

"It can be done," Kevin said. "But Janet and I can't do it alone."

Silence. Finally, Jason spoke. "Well, hell, that comet of mine has come and gone. I might as well do some real work."

"Uh, I'm not really good with a pistol . . ." Bernard swayed in his seat, as if he might pass out.

"Don't worry Bernard," Janet said. "We only have three guns anyway."

Bernard gave a short bark that passed for a laugh, though his face bore no trace of a smile. "Well! I guess that's good news."

"What do you want us to do now?" Angel asked, clutching Kevin's arm.

"Go back in your room," Janet said. "I'll call you when the meeting starts. Then we'll know what to do next."

⁜

Kevin waited until Angel closed the door to speak. He held the gun up. "Okay, we have a chance now."

"We didn't before?"

"No. I thought that if I could go outside the fence, I might buy you some time. Maybe some rescue effort might come along."

"That's stupid," she said.

"It's better than dragging you outside the fence with me. We'd last about thirty minutes out there."

Angel leaned back against the wall. "How long will we last inside? If you can find weapons and secure the windows?"

"We have a chance," he repeated.

⁜

"You all know why we're here," Candice began. The others sat at the workstation or sprawled on the floor. Kevin and Angel stood by the door to their room. Candice had tried to get everyone to sit in a circle, as was their custom, but Kevin and Angel refused, so Candice stayed on her feet as well.

She turned to Kevin directly. "We offered you a trial opportunity here, hoping you would fit into our little community. I'm deeply sorry to say that the experiment has failed."

Kevin stood, arms folded, eyes narrowed to slits. He waited to answer.

"I don't think it failed," Bernard said. His gangly legs uncoiled as he sat forward. "That's my opinion, anyway. And I thought we were supposed to vote this morning. I guess the vote will tell us if it failed or not." He looked down at his hands, which had become twisted

128

together as he spoke.

Candice appeared surprised by Bernard's words. "Yes, of course we're going to vote. All in favor of—"

"Don't you think we should talk about this first? This involves a life. We should discuss this."

Candice stared at Janet. Then her gaze traced through the room. Her face had begun to flush. Her lips tightened. "Certainly." She turned back to Kevin. "Do you have anything to say?"

Kevin took a deep breath. Don't lose your temper, he thought. A glance at Angel almost made him laugh—her eyes were echoing the message. Behave.

He tried to control his voice, but a hint of emotion crept in with a tremor. "I apologize if there are some bad feelings over things I've said. I don't want to insult anyone. But you people are fucking idiots if you think you can pull down the blinds and make the shamblers go away."

Candice tried to interrupt, but Kevin talked over her objections.

"We need to do some things, and we need to do them right away. We need to draw most of those shamblers away from the fence. We need bars for the basement windows and the lobby window. The same thing goes for the windows in the kitchen and dining facility. We can secure most of the lab windows with boards, but those big windows need metal bars. The only way to get what we need to survive is a run into town. We have three guns. I'm suggesting we take three people—four if someone's comfortable with a baseball bat or a crowbar."

"You are supposed to be speaking in your defense!" Candice said, barely controlling her voice.

Kevin pointed at Rod Coleman. "Rod? You're a scientist. I support your work. I don't want to take you away from it. I want to safeguard it." He turned to Wanda next. "Wanda? I don't know a damn thing about parasites. Maybe you're on to something. But how will you research anything if that fence comes down?"

"How many guns will you need?" Candice asked, flushed with anger. "A gun for each of us? Two guns each? If we close the labs down and filled the rooms with bullets, would that be enough? The reason I ask is because there might be 300 million of those things wandering around this country alone. So how many bullets do you need?"

"More than seventy," Kevin answered.

Candice addressed the group. "This is an old game. The answer to that question is always, always more. A thousand? We need more. Ten thousand? The madness never ends. Do you want to feel safe? Find a cure. But you won't cure anything with a gun."

"Dead scientists can't find cures."

"It's clear you don't intend to defend yourself. I'm calling for a vote." Candice clapped her hands for silence, but the room was a riot of voices. Todd Smith asked why only the scientists were important. Wasn't his work important too? Trudy burst into tears. Wanda comforted her, and then turned on Kevin, anger twisting her face. Jason tried to calm the noise, but succeeded only in adding to it.

"People, people, people!" Candice shouted. "This is not who we are!" When the noise subsided, she raised her hand. "All in favor of evicting Kevin and Angel from the group, raise your hand."

Kevin kept his eyes on Coleman. He'd supported the man and tried to drum up assistance for his work. When Coleman raised a hand, something shriveled and fell away inside Kevin. We're all so fucked, he thought.

Candice looked around at the show of hands, frowning. Wanda and Trudy, Coleman, Todd Smith and Candice. "Five votes?"

"Wait a minute!" Lines creased Coleman's forehead. His mouth twisted into a confused frown.

"All opposed?" Kevin asked, raising his arm. Angel, Janet, Bernard, Jason and the Reverend joined him.

"Six votes," Bernard said.

Candice scoffed, pointing at Kevin and Angel. "Well, of course they can't vote. They're the ones on trial here. Measure to evict passes, five to four."

"So much for democracy," Kevin whispered.

"Wait a minute!" Coleman repeated. "I thought we were voting on Kevin, not on the girl."

Janet shook her head. She held up her gun hand, as if to say, wait. She spoke directly to Candice. "You can't ignore their vote. They're residents here, and they get to vote."

"Conditional residents," Candice said. "They did not have full voting privileges."

"Since when?" Angel asked, shaking with anger. "You invited us to live here!"

"A mistake I deeply regret!"

Shouts drowned out Angel's response. Janet put her hand on the butt of the pistol she carried. Kevin shook his head. No. Don't do it. He waved at Candice. "They say you're an entomologist."

"Pardon?"

"You study insects?"

"You need to gather your things and go."

"Corey was studying the rate of rot on the dead," Kevin said, his voice carrying over the arguments that raged around the room. "Like I said, I think everyone's waiting for the shamblers to just disappear. So let me ask your scientific opinion. When spring comes, and the rot accelerates, will they draw flies?"

Candice glared at him in cold fury, without answering.

"Mosquitoes aren't as much of a worry. They prefer to draw living blood. But the flies will be very attracted to the shamblers, don't you think? I wonder what kind of contagions they'll carry on their legs? I wonder if they'll leave any zombie specks in your soup? And they'll lay eggs, of course. I wonder what sort of grubs will burrow out of the flesh? I wonder if they'll still be flies?"

A horrified silence settled over the room.

"And what about cockroaches? Those little guys just love filth and decay."

"What does he mean?" Trudy wailed.

Candice shot her an angry glare and turned back to Kevin. "You're scaring them! You're a dangerous, dangerous man! Thank God we took your gun away! You've been trying to take over this facility since you arrived!"

"If I had a gun, you wouldn't try to evict me," Kevin said.

"If you had a gun, you'd be giving orders!"

Angel grabbed his arm and slumped against him. He looked around the room at the frightened faces. "Look people, you don't have to like me. I'm an asshole sometimes. But seriously, you haven't spent five minutes considering your long-term survival. It's almost too late. Let's start now."

"You've been evicted from the group by a five to four vote," Candice shouted.

"I'm staying. Six to five."

Candice looked to Janet. "You're the security officer! These people have been legally evicted."

Jason Brock stood up. "This is murder, plain and simple. It's not going to happen."

Rod Coleman shook his head. "Candice? I'm not happy with this. There are a lot of those things outside, and I'm not comfortable with just putting them out. Besides, I thought we were voting on the guy, not the girl. Why would we put her out? That would be a death sentence."

"She's pregnant," Candice said.

Coleman shrugged helplessly. "Exactly. We can't evict a pregnant woman. You don't really think they can smell her, do you? Living people don't have a strong sense of smell. I don't think dead people suddenly improve their olfactory. And if they could smell, wouldn't they be more likely to smell a woman's menstrual cycle, rather than the presence of a fetus?"

Candice stared from face to face, weighing what she saw. With her lips pressed tight into a single jagged line, she whirled and went through her bedroom door, slamming it closed behind her. Trudy found a fresh set of tears and ran for the stairway, Wanda following. Coleman looked up at Kevin and shook his head. "I don't know how this got so messed up. Maybe she's right. Maybe mankind deserves what it gets."

"God help us all," the Reverend added.

Kevin scowled. "The Lord helps those that help themselves. He gave us brains. We ought to use them."

Reverend Charles looked away.

Coleman stood up. "This is a very uncomfortable situation," he said, glancing over at Todd Smith for support. "What are we supposed to say to you now?"

"Don't think twice about it," Kevin said. Then he turned to Janet. "I'm going to town. So is Jason. Is there another volunteer?" The room was silent for a moment.

"I'm going, of course," Janet said.

"No. I want you here to get us back through the gate. I don't want to trust our reentry to that guy." He pointed at Coleman.

"I don't blame you. But you need another gun."

"If you clear that gate, I'll grab Corey's pistol. You need to keep yours here." He looked around the room. "How about it, Reverend. Can you swing a crowbar?"

The Reverend shook his head slowly. "This is happening too fast. I wish that we'd have come to some kind of consensus."

"Damn it," Bernard moaned. "I really don't want to do this!"

"I'll go," Angel said.

Kevin laughed. "No offense, babe, but you walk too damned slow. Besides, Janet's going to need someone to watch her back."

Todd Smith shook his head angrily, tossing his graying hair and beard. "You're talking about us like we were traitors. This is our facility! This is our home! You're acting like we're criminals!"

"You just voted to feed a pregnant woman to the living dead," Kevin said, his words soft and clipped, a slight smile trembling on his lips. "You'd better pray I'm a better person than you are."

"You are a thug!" Smith wailed. "Candice was right."

"Shut up." Kevin took a single step toward the man in the Hawaiian shirt. Smith flinched and turned away.

Shouts came from the stairs. Both Trudy and Wanda yelled as they raced down the steps, tripping over each other with their feet and their words. Janet stopped them at the bottom step. "What is it?"

Trudy collapsed in a heap on the steps. Wanda took a deep breath and then pointed up. "They're pushing. They're pushing on the fence!"

Kevin ducked into his room to retrieve the Ruger and the ammo box. The rest of the group ran up the stairs, jostling for space on the narrow passage. Angel sat back against the wall, waiting. "Is this it?" she asked.

Kevin jammed the ammo into his jeans pocket and started for the stairs. "Come on. Let's go see what's happening."

The others had gathered in the lobby. They stood at the blinds, nudging the slats down just enough to see what had happened at the gate. Trudy sat at the receptionist's desk, her head down on the desktop, silent. Kevin walked to the window and grabbed the cord to pull up the blinds, but Todd stopped him. "Don't! They'll see it! Don't rile them!"

Kevin frowned at the others, afraid to look, afraid not to look. Prisoners.

Outside, the shamblers moved forward, a seething mass that bowed the chain link and bent one of the poles forward.

"Those poles are set in concrete, don't you think?" Smith

whispered. "Surely they set them in concrete."

"They put barbed wire on top," Coleman said. "They're not going to put up barbed wire and not anchor the fence poles."

"This is a government-built facility," Bernard said. "Who knows what corners they cut?"

The shamblers surged forward for a moment, creating a bulge in the fence, tilting the loosened pole even further. Then, like a spent wave, the crowd pulled back, and the fence partially righted itself.

"It held. The fence held!"

"Wait."

Most of the shamblers shuffled in place, some bouncing into the chain link. Inside, the watchers held their breath, waiting for another surge that did not come.

"I'm going on the roof," Kevin whispered, backing away. Janet started to go with him, but he shook his head, pointing at the window. "Watch Angel," he mouthed. Janet nodded.

Todd Smith stared at Kevin as he walked down the hall. "Does he have a gun? Where did he get the gun?"

Outside, the shamblers had begun to back away, one or two bouncing forward, another five fading back, the kinetic motion of a drifting cloud.

"Did they give up? Is that what I'm seeing?" Jason's voice was hopeful.

"The fence held. We don't have to go into town. Do we?"

"It's too soon to tell," Coleman said. "They do behave oddly, don't they?" He scratched his chin and squinted through the blinds. "There's clearly some kind of group behavior in play. On some level, they're still social."

"Do you think they have some kind of collective mind?" Wanda asked. She leaned close, pursing her lips into a bow.

"No." Coleman shook his head. "Of course not. I said they're social. That doesn't mean there's any thought involved. It doesn't take any thought to stand in a group."

"How do they know we're here?" Jason muttered.

Coleman rubbed his chin. "I don't think most of them can see.

The eyes go early. I think they can hear a little, though."

"Can they smell babies?"

"I don't think so, Wanda. Can you smell babies?"

"Then why are they hanging around the gate?" Wanda asked in a voice filled with fear and despair.

Coleman shook his head. "I don't know. They're rotting. As they decompose, their ability to perceive is diminished. They're stupid, and they're getting stupider. I expect they'll go away eventually."

"My parasite theory would explain a lot of this."

"Forget all of the theories," Jason said. "The real thing is pushing on the fence."

Kevin came racing up the hallway. He stopped and looked around the room, finding Angel. "We have to leave. Now!" He grabbed her arm and pulled her toward the door.

"What is it?" Janet asked, stricken.

"Come with us!" Kevin ordered. Only Janet followed.

Outside, the morning sun blazed, turning the gray grass into a kaleidoscope of refracted light. The shamblers stared blindly through the fence.

Kevin dragged Angel to the left, around the south side of the building. Two boxes sat in the mud at the southeast corner of the fence. He grabbed the case of granola bars and pitched it back up over the barbed wire. Then, shoving the pistol into his pants, he grabbed the chain link and began to climb. When he reached the top, he grabbed the guidepost that kept the three strands of barbed wire taut and hoisted himself up, dropping over onto the dirt twelve feet below. He stood up and looked into Angel's eyes. "You have to do it now. Don't think."

She began to climb. Her progress was slow, painfully so. Janet looked back. The shamblers were moving again, backing away from the gate. "Climb!" Kevin shouted, but she stood beneath Angel instead, propping her up from behind.

Jason, followed them out onto the grounds, but the sight of so many living corpses froze him. Bernard peered at them from around the corner of the building. When the shamblers pushed at the fence again, they both disappeared.

"Come on, Angel. Come on!" A shambler moved toward them from the north side of the fence, arms outstretched, a mouth smeared with dried blood and flesh. Kevin drew the Ruger and fired, striking the thing in the head, dropping it back into the mud.

Angel reached the top and paused at the barbed wire.

"Grab the post. Step on the fence top."

"It's going to cut me!"

"Pitch yourself over."

"I can't do it!"

"Go! I swear, Angel, I'll catch you!"

Angel pulled herself up. She put one leg on the fence top and slipped. Janet had begun to climb behind her. She pushed from below, holding Angel in place. Bolstered, Angel tried a second time, flipping herself over the wire like a high jumper. Kevin caught her, collapsing in a heap at the base of the fence.

Shamblers closed in. Janet dropped back down inside the fence and pulled her pistol. She squeezed off two shots, dropping one of the dead.

"Come on!" Kevin shouted. "Climb!"

Janet glanced back. The others had gone back into the facility.

"Climb, damn it!"

She stood, staring through the fence, her eyes wide and white, her lips turned down. She met his gaze, and in that moment, her brown eyes told him what he didn't want to know. "I'm so sorry," she said.

Then she ran back to the lobby door.

A naked shambler with a nine-inch tear in his thigh that had festered stumbled forward. Kevin fired twice, striking him in the neck and skull. He flopped down and rolled against the fence.

Other shamblers from the gate were coming. Kevin stood and pulled Angel to her feet.

"My hip!" Angel cried. "Oh my God, it hurts!"

"We move now or we die." Kevin's face was white with terror. The Ruger had three shots left. He patted the ammo box in his pocket. Then he picked up the case of granola. Angel stood up, using the fence as support.

"Can you walk?"

"Help me," she said. She leaned on his right shoulder, transferring some of her weight to him. He looped an arm around her, pulling her away from the fence.

The shamblers almost caught them as they rounded the corner fence post. Angel's hobbled gait slowed them. The dead gained on them with each passing second. "Sweetie, you've got to move faster."

"Leave me!" she wailed, tears squeezing from her eyes.

"Walk, damn it!" Kevin pulled her along, stumbling, each step a potential fall. If I go down, he thought, we both die.

"It hurts!" She rolled her hip as she walked, willing herself across the field. The shamblers came within a few feet of them, a death rattle in their throats, the sound of windpipes full of phlegm and dried blood. Angel cried out loud and began to move faster, swaying with each step, trying not to fall, trying to maintain her balance. Slowly, they began to pull ahead.

And then, as they moved south, across the open field, the shamblers lost interest. The last, a woman who had died in her fifties, dressed in a cotton dress with purple flowers, stopped to look up, staring at the sun, her mouth open and dripping with tan fluids. She reached out to the east, towards town, and then dropped her arms, standing motionless. Instinctively, Angel turned to look. "Oh my God!" she whispered.

Hundreds of shamblers spilled from each intersection along Overland Trail, shuffling their way toward the research facility. Old and young, rotted and fresh, they stumbled forward, drawn by the crowd that surrounded the fence. Joining the others, they surged forward, buckling the chain link in a dozen places. For a moment, it seemed that the fence might still hold. Then a pole gave way on the south side, and a crowd of shamblers crawled over the fence, tripping on the barbed wire, falling forward into the yard.

No longer followed, Kevin stopped to let Angel rest. "Why aren't they after us?" Angel asked.

"So much for smelling babies," Kevin growled. He watched as the residents of the facility appeared on the roof, staring over the edge at the dead below. The west gate came down next, letting a hundred or more shamblers into the compound. They went straight for the research building, arms outstretched, mouths open.

"Where did they all come from?"

Kevin watched, his arms folded across his chest. "There are a hundred thousand corpses in Fort Collins. The real question is, what took them so long?"

"I don't understand."

"It's a flock. One bird flies south, and the others follow."

Janet stood on the south edge of the roof; her hands hand on her hip. Kevin stared, his heart breaking. Why didn't you come with us? he thought. You're trapped, now!"

Janet seemed to know he was watching her. She didn't move for a long while. Bernard came to her side, yapping like a dog, but she ignored him, never breaking her gaze. When Bernard finally drifted away, his arms dangling loose and his head hanging, Janet straightened up, her spine erect, and snapped off a quick salute in Kevin's direction.

Kevin returned the salute and, with an aching soul, turned away.

<hr>

Aside from the intermittent thumping at the door, the sounds of carnage had ceased. Candice stood waiting in the dim morning light, her list of choices reduced to one. And she was unwilling to open the door.

A pair of feet shuffled by the basement window behind her, oblivious to the fragility of glass. For the time being, she was safe. The door wouldn't yield like the fence had. Perhaps Janet would come for her. Surely Janet knew that she was still alive. Janet was in charge of rescue, and she would do her duty. In the meantime, the zombies wouldn't come through the window. They weren't smart enough.

Candice had heard the gunshots and knew what they meant. But by the time she'd grabbed her belongings and made her way into the hall, she found herself facing one of them. A man—or what had once been a man—stood by the door, dressed in hospital clothing, gore splattered the front of the gown like a child's bib at a spaghetti house. She retreated to her room and locked the door.

From inside, she followed the fall of her research facility—the last, best hope for the world gone awry. The sounds of breaking glass, screams and then the hammering blows against the office door all spoke of conflict and finality. "So this is how it ends," she whispered.

She had to go to the bathroom. It was late morning, and a night of sleep and the morning meeting left her bladder crying for release. Soon, she would have to either urinate in the room or burst. She waited. Maybe Janet would come, and they could make a quick stop in the restroom.

Another thump at the door brought tears to her eyes. It was one thing to talk about the end of the world, and quite another to face it. *Oh, if only I knew that men and women would survive*, she decided. The sentiment struck her with heartrending force. She began to cry as a second thought swept the first away. The human race wasn't about to die. She was.

A loud thump at the window turned her like a wind vane in a storm. A pair of boots stood facing her, bumping forward against the glass and then backing away, wandering off towards the facility garden.

Candice covered her eyes with her hands, rubbing them with her palms. *This isn't happening*, she whispered. If only she'd listened to Janet. Janet had wanted to reinforce the windows. She'd wanted to organize a search party and go looking for the necessary building supplies. Candice had refused. To leave the compound and its projects unprotected, even for a few hours, was unthinkable.

And it wouldn't have mattered if it hadn't been for that bitch, Angel. Her and her little ootheca. Candice snarled a small laugh at her private joke—equating the woman's baby with the offspring of an insect. The zombies could smell Angel's child. Candice knew it in her cold bones.

But she'd welcomed Angel and her thug boyfriend into the family, hadn't she? *No good deed goes unpunished*. What else could she have done? Send them off into the night with the last of the facility's groceries? Let their weapons depart? No, she'd done the right thing. But she hadn't known about the baby. She was at the mercy of lies and deception.

The crack of glass was like a knife in her heart. The boots were back, closer, putting a spider web of fissures from frame to frame. Another kick and the glass would tumble into the room, and she would be defenseless.

It won't end this way. She repeated the phrase over and over, but every bump and crack disrupted her chant, rendering it powerless.

I won't be the only one to die. The thought gave her some small satisfaction, but it was bitter compensation for the pain she would suffer. They would bite her, tear at her flesh, and then, long after the pain ended, she would rise and join them.

The others left me here alone. No one was going to rescue her. The realization was devastating. She lay her forehead flush against the door, shuddering. She reached for the doorknob, but could not touch it. *I can't do this! I can't let it end!*

The sound of shattering glass changed her mind. She didn't turn around this time. She pulled the door open and stepped into the main room, whispering, "Let it be done." She ran face-first into the hospital zombie.

The man reeked of rot and vegetables and gas. Blood and tissue hung in clots from his gown. He stared straight ahead without acknowledging her presence. His eyes had clouded over with rheum, pus running from the corners, leaving trails down to his cheeks. As if waking from a deep sleep, he looked at her and opened his mouth.

When he bent down to bite her, the broken shards of his teeth tore a hole in her cheek. The shock took her breath away. She tried to scream, but the sound died in her throat. She threw herself back, slamming her head against the doorframe. Stunned, she stumbled forward, falling to the floor. The zombie's bare legs straddled her face. He bent down and grabbed for her hair. She tried to roll away, but other zombies joined in, and she was engulfed, submerged beneath a crawling mass of dead flesh. Fear ran through her like a convulsion, and she voided her bladder onto the linoleum.

142

A dead woman latched around her leg and pushed her ruined face under the hem of Candice's loose-fitting dress. The bites ran up her thigh in stitches, a seam that left a bloody furrow in her skin. Candice thrashed, but she was already pinned. Teeth dug into the soft flesh of her wrist, snapping and tearing at the tendons. White-hot agony burned the air from her lungs.

The hospital zombie crouched by her head, his gown gaping open behind him. He leaned over her face, pressing the filthy front of the gown into her eyes and nose. She twisted away from the stench of vomit and old teeth, but it followed her, crawling into every orifice.

The woman at her thigh tore a mouthful from her leg, struggling to sever the flesh, shaking her head from side to side until the skin flap tore. At last, Candice could scream—a cry that matched the shrieking agony of being eaten alive. The woman sat back, packing the bloody prize into her cheeks, crimson fluids streaming from her lips. Candice tried to move. Her muscles wouldn't respond.

I'm dying. The thought was but a momentary comfort. The hospital zombie locked his picket-fence teeth on her breast and bit through the dress, cutting into the nipple. He pulled, ripping flesh and dress fabric, unable to tear it loose. Another zombie at her side pushed two decayed fingers into the hole in her cheek. She bit down hard and the fingers burst, shooting putrid liquid down her throat. She gagged, open-mouthed, and the zombie shoved the stumps of his fingers in deeper still.

The hospital zombie fell back, his prize finally dangling between clenched teeth. Candice watched as another tattered zombie fed on fluttering strips of red flesh. She didn't dare look down to see where the feast had come from.

The pain began to subside. I will join them now, she thought. Then the woman at her thigh began to probe in the slit she'd torn open, pushing her fingers into the muscle to the raw nerve cable, ripping it free. Candice sat upright in a single, bright spasm of unimaginable pain, toppling two of the feeding dead. Her back exposed, the zombies moved in closer, biting and scratching at the flower patterns on her spattered dress.

Kevin and Angel moved south, towards the stadium. Angel's hip was tender, but she made good time over the flat fields and the parking lot. She was certain that if she stopped to rest, the hip would stiffen, so she kept moving.

"What's in the box?" she asked at last.

"Granola. We won't starve."

"I wasn't worried about food."

As they closed in on the football field, they noticed odd markings on the sides of the building. The stadium was constructed from a series of gray slabs. Brown markings splashed across the concrete in stark contrast to the flat, neutral colors of the building.

"What the hell?" Angel asked. "What are those?"

The slashes and blotches had no pattern. They covered the walls for a stretch of fifty yards, no more than five or six feet high. Kevin squinted, his head cocked.

"That's dried blood, isn't it?" she asked.

"Zombie art," he whispered.

Angel looked around. The nearest shambler was fifty yards away, wandering aimlessly over the fields of mud. "They're all going to die, aren't they? Those people on the roof?"

Kevin refused to look back. "I don't know." He pulled her away, taking her west, up the road to the reservoir. The winding pavement ahead would go up a steep incline, past the stadium, past scrub and rocks to the dam above Horsetooth Reservoir. From there, they would have a view of the water, the houses that rimmed the reservoir, and the road that led deeper into the mountains.

"Are you okay?" he asked.

"I'm a little winded," she puffed.

"We can rest. We've got a good lead on the shamblers."

She looked back and then shook her head. "My hip is really, really sore. I'm afraid it will lock up."

"The road ahead gets pretty steep."

"I need to keep moving." She took a deep breath and began to walk again. He paced her, reloading the Ruger.

"Want a granola bar?" he asked.

"Later."

"They're peanut butter and chocolate chip," he said.

"I hate peanut butter." She tried to laugh, but the sound died in her throat.

The road curved to the left and rose up into the rocks above. Each step sent a knife's point of pain into her hip. I won't make it up this road, she thought. She tried to shift her weight, rocking from side to side as she moved. It didn't help.

Halfway up, Kevin started laughing. A weak, ugly grin crossed his face. "Say, remember how everyone was so fired up about not repeating mankind's mistakes?"

"Yeah," Angel puffed. Despite the morning chill, a stinging sweat rolled into her eyes.

"Well, it seems to me like we repeated one of the oldest mistakes of all. We underestimated an indigenous population."

"I don't get it."

"Bad joke. It doesn't matter." He continued to climb, the box of granola bars on one shoulder. "But if you want to avoid the mistakes of the past, you should identify them first."

They moved into a pass above the stadium. Kevin could see the research facility in the distance, but couldn't discern anyone on the roof. As he walked, trees blocked the view. *Just as well,* he thought. *Goodbye, Janet.*

Angel trudged up the hill, gasping with each step. She stopped twice on her way to the top, leaning on her good leg, her head on his shoulder. A single shambler followed them, distracted, his head fixed firmly to the left as if someone had broken his neck at the moment of his death. A trail of brown dribbled over his left shoulder and down the side of his shirt. They had sixty yards on the dead man. It was plenty.

Ahead, the road rose to the rim of the reservoir.

"Just a few more steps," Kevin promised. "Then we'll see what's what, and we'll decide what to do next."

Angel pushed ahead, step by painful step. "I hope there's a place we can rest."

"I'm sure of it," Kevin promised. "Most of the houses up here have well water. We'll stop and get something to drink. How does that sound?" He dragged her along without waiting for an answer. They reached a T-intersection at the lip of the reservoir. The road north, to the right, crossed over the dam and rose up above the reservoir. Angel's hip would not make the climb. They went south instead.

"Not much further." He pulled her along, just steps now from the ridge where he could see the south end of the reservoir. *I'll look it over and decide what's best. I'll know what to do.*

"You won't let them eat me, will you?" she asked.

They stepped up over the curb and crossed twenty feet of soft grass to the edge of the cliff. They stood, silent. A breeze drifted across the rim, smelling of green shoots and wet soil—hints of spring.

He gripped the pistol. "Don't worry," he whispered.

AUTHOR'S NOTE

And that's how it ends. Let me recap the action: Angel asks Kevin not to let her be eaten by the zombies. He puts his hand on his pistol and tells her not to worry. You can figure it out easily enough.

But to my surprise, some readers still wondered what happened next. I thought I'd made it perfectly clear. But it was not clear, and it was not perfect. There were some unfinished themes that left loose ends dangling like tendons from a severed wrist.

And, as it happens, I had a vague idea for a sequel in the back of my head. My publisher might demand a follow-up. (It could happen.)

Suppose my protagonists found shelter? What would the world look like in six months? What would the constant stress do to Kevin and Angel? And what about the baby? I decided to exorcise the nagging questions with a short story. I sat down and started writing, and when I looked up, I'd written a novella.

Call it closure. Call it "Dread Appetites."

So let's pretend for a moment that Kevin didn't shoot Angel and then himself at the top of the ridge overlooking Horsetooth Reservoir. If you wanted more, here it is. But be careful what you wish for.

The grocery store entryway was black, like a dead, open mouth. The sun couldn't penetrate the windowless interior of the building. Kings Soopers had been a twenty-four hour operation before the Apocalypse. Now, broken glassware and the dried remnants of food littered the front walk. A soft breeze nudged a wrapper stuck to the sidewalk by a sauce that hadn't always been a brown crust.

The breeze smelled clean. It felt good on his neck. No hint of death. The man sat with his arms wrapped around his knees, watching. He turned to look back every few moments. Otherwise, he was still. The hot summer had carried over into fall. *Global warming,* he thought. The small joke, the cool breeze and a moment to rest had a strange effect on him; a smile crossed his lips.

"No," he whispered, and the smile was gone. He had a job to do. He stood up, checked the sidewalk behind him again and walked to the entryway. He carried an empty backpack, a flashlight in one hand and a Ruger .44-caliber in the other. When he switched on the light, the beam shook along with his hand.

He crept into the store, his ears tuned to the smallest sound, pausing every few steps, playing the beam across the empty shelves. When he found the aisle he was looking for, he took a deep breath and moved ahead. There were only two ways out of an aisle. If both ways became blocked, he would be in trouble.

Sweat ran down his forehead. He stopped to wipe his eyes, but a sound froze him in place. A footstep? He waited for another sound. Silence.

The shelves were stripped of everything but some rattles and a few tubes of Vaseline. He pocketed the Vaseline and moved on. A familiar despair settled in. Had everything been taken?

On his way out, he made certain to check the back of the bottom shelves. Near the aisle cap, he found what he was looking for. Five cans! He stooped to grab them, hand extended. With his fingers on the cans, he paused to listen. He could hear the shuffling from the other side of the aisle.

He pulled the first can from the back of the shelf and set it on the ground. Reaching, his fingers shook, and he dropped the second can on the metal rack, a sound so loud that he jumped. A rattle and hiss came from the adjacent aisle, followed by a bump against the shelving.

Kevin scooped the remaining cans into a pile, groaning with frustration. He heard steps from just beyond the end of the aisle, no more than six feet away. He stood, shaky flashlight in hand, and pulled the hammer back on the Ruger.

The shambler turned the corner, one gray eye locked on the flashlight's beam. The rest of the thing's face was a mess of rot and webbing, home to insects and grubs. Its mouth opened to reveal a few broken teeth stained black with the tar of its last meal. It reached forward, fingers stripped to bone, moving slowly, twitching like an insect caught in sap. Kevin let the hammer down without firing and clubbed the shambler with the barrel. It staggered and fell, twitching for a moment before going still.

The urge to grab the cans and run was almost overwhelming. Instead, he stood still, listening. He tucked his shaky hands under his armpits, clamping them to his sides.

No more sounds. He removed his backpack and shoveled the five cans of soybean infant formula inside. He checked the shelves one last time, looking for anything he could use, and moved back down the aisle. Despite the urge to run, he forced himself to creep and to listen. At the far side of the aisle, he peered around the end cap and headed for the door. When he stepped into the sunlight, he gasped with relief. He'd been holding his breath for a while.

He checked behind to make sure he hadn't been followed, a habit he would have for the rest of his life. Then he paused for just a moment, weighing the idea of trying another grocery store. He could move east and catch the Safeway in the middle of town, but it would mean at least two more hours on the road.

Instead, he made his way north toward a convenience store and a gas station. From there, he'd head west, past the old research facility. He'd check one more thing off of his list and then he'd go home.

The King Soopers was only his second grocery store. He'd looted the Safeway on Taft and Drake earlier in the week, coming away with two plastic bottles and a package of disposable diapers. Finding the formula today was like hitting the jackpot. He already knew the convenience store and the grocery store wouldn't have anything for him. But with a good find tucked safely in his pack, he could afford to catch up on old business.

The summer heat had been brutal to the undead, slowing them to a crawl, rotting them until they couldn't move anymore. Some of them just disappeared.

He'd only fired the Ruger once in the last two months. A fresh shambler, recently dead, had surprised him while he searched the cars on Overland. His shot, fired in panic, clipped the shambler's skull. Kevin finished the thing off with a crowbar.

He found one shambler under a car. The thing's legs had fallen off. It had been crawling on concrete, stripping the flesh from its palms and belly. It lay beneath the chassis, head turned to face him, its mouth opening and closing. Kevin left it alone.

Once, a month after leaving the research facility, Kevin saw some living humans. A battered pickup truck crawled along the fields adjacent to Overland carrying two men in the truck bed, armed with shotguns. Kevin had been foraging. He crawled under a car and waited until the pickup was gone. Then he rushed home to make certain that the truck hadn't gone to the reservoir. Climbing the road, he saw the truck in the distance, off to the south, heading back into town. He sighed his relief and returned to the cars on Overland.

Now, two blind shamblers fumbled at the broken glass door of the convenience store, cutting away at their arms and clothing. Kevin decided to move on without going inside.

The gas station at the corner of Mulberry and Taft had been picked clean. There were no shamblers in sight, so Kevin went through the motions of checking drawers and the dark bottoms of shelves. He searched the garage bay, hoping for a few tools, but even those were gone. He left the station behind and headed west. He'd been this way before, six months earlier, dragging Angel through streets of carnage. The same cars blocked the road. He hadn't mined these for food. Instead, he'd revisited Overland Trail, month after month, even when the pickings had become slim.

One afternoon, late in the summer, he returned with just a half-sleeve of saltines to show for his day. Angel sat him down and took his hand. "We need to try something else," she said. "We're running out of food, and the baby will be here soon."

"You want me to try cars on other streets?" he asked.

She stared at him for a moment, as if he frightened her. "I mean we need to see what's left in the stores."

He mulled the idea over for a day. "I've been thinking about this," he told her in a cracked, halting voice. He'd lost the habit of speaking. There hadn't been much to say. "I think I feel safe working the cars on Overland. It's something I've done, so it's what I do." He paused and looked into her eyes. "Even with everything that's happened, I think I ended up like Jason and Wanda. Remember how they kept after their research instead of doing something useful? I guess I didn't learn a thing from what happened."

During the first months of the Apocalypse, Kevin and Angel had taken sanctuary in a small research facility on Overland Trail. The scientists inside were supposed to be working on a cure for the zombie uprising. In the end, they focused on their pet theories, avoiding the hard work of survival. They hadn't attended to the defense of the facility, and when a zombie attack pushed down the fence, they were doomed.

"I know you're doing your best. We're both frightened," Angel said. But that wasn't right. He wasn't frightened, not like he had been. The fear had been burned out of him. What was left was the dry husk of paralysis.

He promised her that he would branch out, try some of the groceries and hardware stores on the west end of town. The shamblers were less of a threat now that rot had begun to claim them. But as each day came, he found himself on Overland Trail again, crowbar and Ruger in hand. He began to lie about where he'd been and what had happened to the hours between dawn and sunset. Weeks slipped away.

Then, just days earlier, he found her in the kitchen at dawn, staring out the bay window at the reservoir below, fingers to the glass, tears running down her cheeks. "What's wrong?" he asked. She wouldn't answer him. He asked again and sat down to hear the answer that never came. She wouldn't look at him. He waited for a long while before leaving. That morning, he tried the first grocery.

She cried when she saw the baby bottles and diapers.

Ahead, he could see the research facility. The fence around the south side remained smashed and broken, a grim reminder of what had happened. When they'd abandoned the place, there had been a hundred shamblers pounding at the windows. Now, the yard was empty.

Kevin tried not to look too closely as he approached. Instead, he kept his eyes on the houses to either side, watching out for stray shamblers.

On his scavenging trips, Kevin still saw groups of shamblers, but there were seldom more than a dozen. Once, he saw four dead men stumbling over the field to the north of the stadium, all with damaged feet and legs, hobbling together at the same snail's pace. He imagined that they'd once been part of a bigger group, breaking into a smaller party because they couldn't keep up with the herd.

He reached Overland and crossed the street, watching between cars and behind every bumper—anywhere but up. When he came to the lawn he stopped and turned his gaze to the roof.

She was there waiting, a silhouette against an orange sun. *Where else would she be? Shamblers are too stupid to open a hatch. They're trapped up there.* He shook his head and groaned. *By God, they were too stupid to open the hatch when they were alive.*

He pointed the Ruger at her, lining up the pistol's sites with her head, but the sun was bright and his eyes began to weep. He moved south, and she followed him along the rim of the roof. He tried again, out of the sun's glare, but again tears prevented him from a sure shot.

Her name was Janet. She'd been a security guard before the Apocalypse. She'd been in charge of the facility's defenses. But there were too few weapons, not enough ammunition, and when the shamblers came, she was just another victim.

She had been his friend.

I could go up there, he thought. He weighed the idea and dismissed it in the same instant. *This is a fool's errand anyway. I must be crazy! When I fire this shot, I'll draw attention.* He wasn't worried about shamblers. He could outrun them. But the idea of drawing the attention of the living frightened him.

Meanwhile, the wreck that had once been Bernard joined Janet at the roof's edge. When the shamblers pulled down the fence, everyone inside the facility had taken refuge on the roof. That was where they died. That was where they'd been resurrected. Bernard had been the group's computer expert. A summer in the sun had destroyed his slender frame. He looked like a skeleton dressed in rags.

Fuck this. Kevin raised the gun again and squeezed off a single shot. The woman pitched back out of sight.

Kevin turned away and began to walk. He glanced back after a few moments. No one followed. In his mind, he could still hear the echoes of the shot bouncing off the mountain ridges. *Sleep, Janet.*

One more task completed. With today's work, the only real job left at hand was food for the baby. When he found enough, he could—

What? He'd been tying up loose ends and settling his affairs.

Saying his goodbyes. That was a bad sign.

He picked up his pace. Angel would be worried. If she could still walk, he'd gladly take her along. But they'd jumped the fence to leave the research facility. She'd landed wrong, and her hip had never really healed. With their baby ready to come, she had trouble getting around the house.

Passing the stadium, he checked the blood spatters again. He'd been watching the patterns for six months. Sure enough, there were new ones. The giant "mural" covered the north end of the stadium from one end to the other. Kevin could make out images—people eating other people, a cross, a Jesus figure being eaten by what appeared to be shamblers and people on their knees, begging.

At first, the drawings had been splotches.

Then, one day he saw the straight lines of the familiar symbol that he'd always thought of as a comfort—the cross. *The shamblers have turned into artists.* He didn't tell Angel, not until weeks later when the mural expanded and took on a cautionary feel. There was a pattern to the images. Fat figures consumed thin ones. A crowd of skeletons chewed on the Messiah. It was hard to interpret.

By then, he'd decided that humans—living ones—were doing the painting. He supposed some people took refuge in the stadium. It frightened him to think so, and he took a wide turn when passing the building, afraid of snipers. The world had gone crazy at the end. The safest thing to do was hide.

As the baby's due date approached, Kevin considered exploring the stadium and trying to contact the people inside. But if they were still there, and he contacted them, they might kill him. He couldn't risk leaving Angel alone.

She wasn't there to greet him when he came through the door. He shouted for her. His voice echoed through the loft-style home. Then silence.

He gripped the rail of the walkway and scanned the living room and kitchen below. The house was clean, nothing out of place. He circled the walkway, fifteen feet above the main floor, checking every corner from above. She wasn't downstairs. He turned to the right—to the closed bedroom door. *She's asleep; she's asleep,* he repeated. He grabbed the doorknob and turned it. Unlocked.

He cracked the door. "Angel? Are you all right?"

The door jerked open. She stood gasping, red-eyed and disheveled. Her thin blonde hair spilled off to the side, matted with sweat. She smelled like sour milk. He stepped back.

"Where have you been?" she demanded.

"Hunting. I found some formula." He pulled off his backpack and began to fumble with the snap. His hands shook.

"The baby's coming." She smoothed the white tee shirt over her belly.

"Today?"

"Now." She grabbed his hand and pulled him into the bedroom. She'd set clean towels and a water basin on the nightstand, along with rubber bands, scissors and a needle and thread. "The scissors and needle have been sterilized," she said, limping over to the bed.

"I could have done this for you."

"You weren't here. I didn't know if you'd be back. I never do." She bit off the end of each word. Stopping at the edge of the bed, she turned and sat down. Falling back into the mattress, groaning, she slid under the covers.

"I found formula."

"I heard you."

Kevin scowled.

"Kevin! I'm scared and I hurt all over. I thought I was going to have to do this alone!" She slammed her head back into the pillow and closed her eyes. When she spoke again, her voice had softened. "What kind of formula?"

"Soybean."

"Is that good?"

"Five cans good."

"Five cans? How long will that last?"

"Not long. But I'll find more—"

She interrupted him with a moan. She pushed back against the pillow and cried out, her hands gripping the sheets as if the bed were trying to crawl out from under her. He watched, silent as stone, until the contraction faded. At last, she wiped her eyes and looked at him again. "Are you all right?"

"It's hard to watch," he mumbled. "There's not a lot I can do for you."

She nodded. "Just be here."

He grabbed a chair from the corner of the room and placed it next to the bed. "I'm here. Do you have any idea how long we have?"

"The contractions are two minutes apart."

"Holy crap."

"Yes."

He took her hand and rubbed it.

"I'm going to scream," she warned. She had been warning him for weeks. "I'm a big baby about pain."

"It's okay," he said. "I don't care."

"I'm glad the waiting is over. Worrying is just too hard." She pushed the hair from her forehead. Her face was dry skin, stretched over bone. "I just want to be done."

When the next contraction came, her eyes bulged out as if they might pop loose from her sockets and spill across her cheeks. Kevin had to turn away. She'd been beautiful once. Six months hiding in the house left her an aged cripple.

Did I ever love her? He couldn't tell. He'd wanted her. She was his boss, untouchable. Then came the Apocalypse. She'd said once that she didn't know how anyone could love anyone in a world ruled by the living dead. He hadn't understood then. He did now.

It's not love. It's something different. He *needed* her. They didn't talk. They didn't make love. They couldn't comfort each other. But when she inhaled, he exhaled. *I need her. It's as simple and pathetic as that.*

She grabbed his hand, squeezing until it hurt. When the grip relaxed, she let out a huge sigh. "Don't be angry with me."

"I'm not."

"I mean, don't be angry when I tell you this."

"Tell me what?" She looked at him with sad affection, tears at the corners of her eyes. The woman he'd cared about was inside that broken shell. He felt ashamed.

"Something's wrong with the baby, Kevin."

The first time Angel mentioned her fears about the baby, Kevin ignored her. This was her first child. Hospitals and doctors were a thing of the past. Of course she was scared. "You didn't know this about me, but I took some courses when I was in college," he said. "It's been years, but I actually know some things about delivering babies. Giving birth is a natural process that usually takes care of itself. And if something goes wrong, I have a pretty good idea what to do."

He'd lied, trying to put her mind at ease. He'd taken a first aid course once. And while working part-time as a taxi driver, he'd read up on assisting a birth. *Wouldn't it be cool if I had to deliver a baby?* It was a daydream, worth fifteen minutes of fun reading. He remembered enough of the information to sound like someone who knew something.

Angel was not comforted. "I mean there's something wrong inside," she said.

"What do you mean? Are you spotting? A little blood is

normal."

"That's not what I mean."

"What then?"

"I can't explain it. I just know."

Her answer made him angry; a helpless fury that returned, full-force as she gripped the mattress in the bedroom, trying to deliver. He pulled the bedspread aside and slipped the bottom of the tee shirt up.

"Did you wash your hands?" she groaned.

He bit his lip and backed away.

"Hurry."

He went down to the living room to wash his hands. He needed to be away for a moment, to catch his breath. The house had its own well, one of many attractions. He scrubbed his hands twice, clean to the forearms. Then he walked to the dining room window, arms extended, and stood while his hands dried in the air. A towel would contaminate them.

He could see the reservoir seventy-five feet below. The house had been built into the side of the mountain. The front door was the only opening on the side of the house that faced the road. The other side of the house faced the cliff. From the front, the house looked to be no more than ten feet tall. Anyone with a chair could climb up on the roof.

Once inside, on the walkway that ringed the second floor, the house looked different. Exposed beams and lights hung twenty-five feet above the living room. The west wall featured a series of huge windows that faced the steep drop to the rocks and water below.

The only way into the house was the front door and a small window near the northwest corner of the house. Kevin had walled up the outside corner with cinderblocks and barbed wire taken from a construction site up the road. That had been one of the items on his to-do list.

"Are you coming back?" she called from above.

He didn't answer.

When they left the research facility, they planned to move deeper into the mountains, looking for a safe place. But when they'd reached the lip of the reservoir, Kevin realized that Angel's hip would prevent her from going much farther. The marina at the south end of the reservoir crawled with shamblers. He gave a brief thought to trying to get a boat out into the water, but he didn't know a thing about boats, and he'd have to come to shore for food eventually.

Instead, he began checking doors. Their present home was the second place he checked. The door was locked, but after peeking under the welcome mat, he found a spare key on the frame above the door. He made Angel stand on the driveway while he went inside. It took him four rounds to make the house safe and fifteen minutes more to clear the mess. She stood shivering in the morning sun. One shambler came shuffling past while he worked. She called to him twice, and when he didn't answer, she shrieked for him. He strode out, gun in hand, just as the shambler reached for her.

Later, huddled in the dark in their new home, he told her how angry she'd made him. "What if I hadn't come out? Would you have let the thing bite you?"

"You didn't answer me!"

"You have to survive, with or without me. You can't count on me. I told you that." He tapped his temple with one finger. "There's something broken in here."

She answered, "The whole world is broken." Now she was calling to him again from the room upstairs.

He rubbed his eyes with his forearms to keep his hands sanitary. *God, give me a second! This is happening too fast! Give me a minute and let me breathe!*

"Kevin!" Her cry ripped through him like teeth.

He took the stairs two at a time. She met him at the bedroom door, gasping. "The baby!"

"I'm here," he said.

Angel watched his face.

"When the contractions come again, don't push." He put a hand on her belly. "You've seen this on television. You puff, puff, puff. It will help keep you from pushing."

"The baby wants to come," she said. Her face was sallow, bathed in sweat. She twisted in the sheets, legs splayed, her tee shirt pulled up to the middle of her stomach.

"I know," he said. She locked her gaze on his eyes, nodding to everything he said, hearing none of it. Blood pounded in her ears,

163

thundering like the drums of a marching band, pushing the baby forward. *Let it be over. Let it all be over!* She pushed.

He shook his head, no. "The baby will come too quickly if you don't pause during the contractions."

She nodded and pushed.

The baby had crowned. She could feel it. Kevin stood at her side, his hands between her legs. *He's holding the baby's head,* she thought. *Thank God, thank God! He knows what he's doing. Oh, Kevin!*

"The baby's head is out," he told her. "I'm trying to get one shoulder out." He grimaced. She focused on his expression. She'd know if something was wrong from his expression.

"Ah."

She pushed again.

"Wait, wait!" he ordered. His voice was firm, not angry. He lifted the baby up a little and smiled. It was a beautiful smile, the smile of a child. She hadn't seen a smile on his face in six months. Tired and in pain, she found herself smiling back. *He's so handsome when he smiles!*

"I have the shoulders. One more push, okay?"

She pushed.

"Oh. Oh!" He pulled the baby free. She searched his eyes. He was crying now. "Oh, she's so pretty!" He looked up, his gaunt face etched with emotion. "We have a daughter."

"Is she all right?"

Kevin grabbed a towel and began wiping the baby's face. He seemed focused now, his eyes locked on the unseen bundle. No expression, just an intense gaze and a sense of purpose.

"I can't hear her cry. Is she breathing?"

He looked over. "She's fine. She's just—" He stopped.

"What's wrong with her?"

"Nothing," he insisted. He leaned forward, staring. "You're crowning again."

"What are you talking about?"

He looked up and met her gaze. "Twins. We're having twins."

"Oh my." She felt the onset of another contraction. "How are we going to take care—" A sharp, piercing pain cut her short.

"Try not to push, Angel." He looked up, flashed a brief smile and turned back to the task, his forehead creased with lines of deliberation. He began to mutter. "Too fast, too fast." He leaned in closer.

"What's wrong?"

He frowned. "Nothing. But you have to stop pushing during the contractions. Breathe."

"I'm not pushing now. The contraction stopped."

He shrugged and leaned in closer. "The head is out. Christ, you're a natural baby factory. You're popping them out. The shoulder is free."

"Are you going to cut the cords?"

"Not right away," Kevin said. He lifted the second baby up, cradling its head, in order to free the other shoulder. Then he leaned in closer. She found herself watching his face again. He squinted. "It's a boy. One boy and one girl." He turned the baby in his arms.

Then he froze.

She saw his face change, and her insides turned. He dropped the baby on the sheets and stood up, wiping his hands on his shirt.

"Kevin?"

He stared down at the baby, his face etched with disgust. His pupils were black holes. He shook once, a sudden convulsion.

"Kevin!"

He backed away for a moment, frantically searching the room. He grabbed something from the dresser.

"What's wrong?"

He turned, a knife in one hand. "Lay still." His voice was thin and brittle. "I'm going to take care of the cords now."

"What's wrong with my baby?"

He ignored her. His skin had yellowed, like thin parchment, aging him by a decade. *It's a trick of the light,* she thought.

"I'm going to tie off the two cords," he said. "Then I'm going to cut them. I'm going to have you breast feed. That will help you expel the placenta."

She fell back against the pillow, spent. *So dizzy! The room is spinning!* In a few moments, Kevin put one of the babies on her stomach. Her daughter—a beautiful daughter. She would call her Jessica. Kevin helped her pull the tee shirt up, exposing a breast. Jessica began to feed.

"Where's my son?"

Kevin bent down again, scooping something into a blanket. "He didn't make it."

Outside, Kevin dumped the bundle on the driveway. The package moved in fits and starts, as if someone had wrapped a dying cat in cloth. The thing smelled of body fluids and excrement and rot. When he'd touched it, part of the boy's skin had sloughed off in his hands. Still born. The baby was still born.

He went back inside to grab what he needed. He thought he heard Angel call again. He ignored her and returned to the driveway. The shovel felt heavy in his hands. He lifted it over his head and swung down hard.

The bundle still moved.

He swung again, slamming the flat of the blade against the thing's head. The blow sounded like a hammer striking a watermelon. The bundle stopped moving.

"Kevin Junior," he whispered.

When he returned, the placenta had been expelled. It lay in a bloody puddle between her legs. She wept, the baby at her breast. Kevin pulled a chair to her side and sat holding her hand. Through the window on the west wall, he saw the sun slip down over the mountaintop, bathing the reservoir in splashes of yellow and orange. Pines and cottonwoods reflected the hues of the red cliffs.

"I'm a mess," she said.

"I'll clean you up in a moment." He draped the bedspread over her legs and stomach, covering the baby.

"Are you okay?"

He considered the question.

The baby began to cry, the raw sound of complaint. It was a healthy sound.

"Her name is Jessica."

"I thought we might call her Brittany."

"No, no." Angel's voice drifted, a puff of smoke in the dying light. "There are a million girls named Brittany."

"This is the last baby," Kevin answered.

They were still. The sun dropped behind the mountains, turning the sky from blue to indigo to black. Cloud cover blanketed the stars. Kevin considered going to the kitchen to make some rice, but decided against it.

"Kevin?"

He squeezed her hand.

"Do you love our daughter?"

He laid his head against her, tears rolling from his eyes.

"Do you love me?"

He tried to answer. His throat was sore with emotion.

"I want you to promise me. Promise me that you'll take care of Jessica."

He nodded.

"I'm very tired."

He swallowed a sob.

"I'm so sorry to leave you like this." Her voice cracked. "I feel so weak."

"It's normal," he said. "You don't know. This was your first baby."

"Babies."

"Yes."

He nestled his head closer, burrowing against her side. He could hear the baby sucking again. She didn't cry. Good baby.

"Kevin?"

He didn't answer. He lay still. Later, when he realized that she was gone, he wished that he'd said something. He might have told her how much he loved her. He might have kissed her lips one last time and let her slip away with his eyes on her. He might have parceled out promises. Or he might have begged her to stay with him. Instead, he'd been silent.

He pulled the baby from her breast. He couldn't risk leaving her there. Sooner or later, Angel would turn. And she would want to feed.

He took his daughter downstairs. He piled two blankets on the couch that faced the big window and wedged the baby against the cushions. Jessica whimpered for a few minutes and then went to sleep. Kevin stood in the dark, listening to her breathe.

A thump from upstairs warned him.

Angel was up and moving.

He crossed the room. He'd left the Ruger on the counter. He tapped his hands across the stone surface, searching for the gun.

When he found it, he swallowed and headed for the stairway.

The moon had risen over the mountains, throwing a gray light across the loft rail. He climbed the steps, one by one. Another bump came from the bedroom. He kept the gun pointed forward. If she came at him, he'd fire. He would shoot her once in the sternum and then put a bullet in her head.

At the top of the stairs, he put a hand to the wall. He crept along, listening. He heard another sound, this one closer to the bedroom door.

This is it, he thought. *This is what you've been dreading.* He reached the bedroom door, turned the knob and pushed it open. The door bumped into someone just inside. He could see Angel's dark shadow, moving forward.

He nearly pulled the trigger. But she moved like molasses, each step a hitch and slide. Her hip slowed her to a crawl. He backed away and let her follow. Her arms rose, begging for an embrace, something he wanted more than anything he could think of. He backed toward the front door, pulling it open.

Two shamblers stood waiting on the lawn. He nodded in their direction. They waited like statues.

Step, slide. Step, slide. She reached the doorway. The moonlight lit her hair like a halo. She crept outside, her arms still extended. Blood coated her legs.

Kevin raised the Ruger, still backing away. A glance behind told him the shamblers hadn't moved. He darted around her and shut the door. Then he ran back down the driveway. Angel followed him, past the dark blanket bundled on the asphalt. He led her beyond the shamblers, down to the road. One of the shamblers joined her as she shuffled forward. The dead man had a torn kneecap. Its shredded pants were coated with black gore. They moved together, shuffling in step, chasing him north. The other shambler stood rooted to the lawn.

Kevin pulled back the hammer on the Ruger.

She closed in, rolling her hip as she walked, mouth open. "Goodbye," he whispered.

His finger tensed on the trigger. She was on him, teeth to the barrel.

When he was down to one can of formula, he decided to venture out again. Angel had fashioned a baby knapsack out of a blanket with a needle and some fishing line. He would hitch the baby sack to the front and his backpack to the rear. That would leave his arms free for the Ruger and his crowbar. As dangerous as that was, he couldn't imagine leaving the baby alone.

Jessica had answered a question that had dogged him for months. What does a person live for when the world ends? Angel's death should have finished him too, but the baby needed him. Her helplessness awakened something in him. *I have to survive. No matter what the cost.*

He left the house at dawn. He wanted plenty of time to cross town to another grocery store, grab whatever was available and head back. And he wanted to be able to take the long way around what ever he came across. *If I see her, I'll go the opposite direction. I couldn't bear seeing her now.* He hadn't been able to shoot her.

The day after Angel passed away, Kevin dug a small grave for the blanket on his driveway. He scooped the bundle up with the shovel and put it in the hole, dreading any sign of motion, thankful when it didn't happen.

When he reached the road to the football stadium, he turned right, heading to the south end of town. Jessica was quiet for the first hour. When she began to cry, finally, he stopped to change and feed her. He'd brought diapers and the rest of the formula in the backpack, enough for two days. If he became trapped for some reason, he wouldn't have to scramble to care for her.

As he walked, he leaned down to kiss the top of her head. He had to remind himself to touch her, to talk to her. He didn't want her to grow up disconnected. She was already motherless. He imagined her as a teen, angry, lost and rebellious. It was the most comforting image he could conjure.

As he approached College Avenue, the main street running through Fort Collins, Colorado, he encountered more shamblers. They moved too slowly to worry over. What frightened him was the chance of a bite or scratch from a random shambler under a car or behind a bumper. And cars were everywhere. He had to be vigilant, something that took every ounce of his energy.

Rotted shamblers occupied some of the cars. They pressed close to the windows, blood and bits of skin painting the inside of the glass, marking the motion of creatures too stupid to pull the handles on the doors. The stench of rancid meat and the drill-bit whine of fat, green flies turned Kevin's stomach. Jessica nestled close to him, a quiet, urgent reminder of the task at hand.

The grocery store, an Albertson's, had been picked nearly clean. He found a small box of rice cereal, but Jessica wouldn't be eating solid food for months. He turned north, walking up College Avenue, dodging the shamblers that drifted over the pavement graveyard.

A group of twenty shamblers stood at the door to a corner gas station. Kevin's first thought was, *Someone's living in there!* But closer inspection revealed broken windows and no place to hide. The shamblers had gathered together, a mindless flock without a shepherd. Kevin crept by, trying not to make much noise. The dead never glanced his way.

The second grocery store was another King Soopers. This one was closer to the center of town, so he had slender hope for supplies. He was pleasantly surprised.

There were plenty of boxes on the shelves. In fact, there was enough food to warrant multiple trips back. How could that be? He'd shopped in the store before the Apocalypse. It had always been crowded. He imagined the crush of people in the final days, fighting over the food. Perhaps the fighting had taken precedence over the looting.

Jessica gave him a start inside the store. She began to cry when he knelt to put formula cans in his backpack. The sound was raw and throaty, echoing through the darkened store. But the shamblers inside couldn't seem to locate him from the sound. On his way out, he spotted one facing a corner, scuffling its feet, trying fruitlessly to walk through a wall.

On the way home, Kevin felt a brief moment of calm. He had six more cans of formula—not the same brand as the first five cans, but formula nonetheless. He chuckled at the idea of post-apocalyptic brand loyalty. Then the sound of his brittle laugh sobered him. He thought of Corey and Janet, the last friends he might ever have.

And he thought of Angel. The smile died on his face, coming back moments later in the form of tears.

He dreaded the last half hour of the trip. If he crossed Angel's path, he would run. All the way up the hill to the reservoir's edge, he watched, dreading the sight of a limping corpse with blonde hair.

He saw three figures at the front of his house the moment he crested the hill. One of them could barely walk. Jessica began to cry again. He covered her head with his palm, stroking her. She'd been so good, so patient! He had to get home. He reached down and cocked the Ruger. If he had to fire, he'd put the crowbar under his arm and clamp his free hand over the baby's ears.

With luck, he'd outrun them instead.

Closer now, he saw that one of the three was a blonde. The realization dismayed him, enough so that it didn't register that one of the figures was screaming.

Screaming. One of them was alive.

He ran, the baby bouncing against his chest with each step. Now, another shouted, "Help us! Hurry!"

Kevin pulled up short. He had only a moment to sort out the scene in front of him. A shambler had closed to within a yard of one of the women—a brunette who seemed to be having trouble walking. The other, a blonde, stood pointing and screaming. The shambler opened its mouth, revealing a few broken teeth inside a black mouth.

Kevin was too far away for the crowbar. He dropped it, covered Jessica's ears and fired the Ruger. The shambler stumbled back, dropping to the pavement.

"Get away from it," Kevin called. He'd gone for the thing's torso, a surer shot. It would get back up in a moment.

The blonde grabbed the brunette and tried to lead her away. "Where can we go?" she called. "Do you have a safe place?" The shambler sat back up, a hole through its chest. Had it been a man or a woman? The creature wore shredded jeans and a tee. Half of its hair had been torn out. There was no way to tell the gender from the ruined face.

"Please?" called the blonde. He didn't answer.

"Mister, I can't walk much farther." The brunette's tiny voice sounded desperate.

He thought of Janet. He'd needed a sanctuary once.

The shambler struggled to its feet.

Angel, what do I do?

"It's getting up!" the blonde shrieked.

Kevin picked up the crowbar and strode forward. The two women limped to the side of the road, their gazes locked on the shambler.

The shambler turned to them, taking a tentative step, but by then Kevin reached it, swinging the steel bar, blasting its skull into pulpy shards. The shambler stumbled and fell, shaking on the pavement for a full twenty seconds before coming to rest.

"There's more coming," the blonde warned. The shot had drawn two more shamblers from the south. Kevin pointed up his driveway. "That's my house," he said. "Let's get inside."

He took them to the door and pulled out his key. The two shamblers moved closer, step by halting step, but they would not reach them in time. He opened the door and ushered the women in. Inside, he locked the deadbolt and took a deep breath.

"Oh my God," the blonde said, staring out over the sunken living room and kitchen. "This place is beautiful!" She gripped the loft rail with both hands, as if the sight of the house was too much to bear. When she glanced back, her face startled him. She might have been pretty once, but she was too thin now. Her cheekbones jutted out like points, and her cheeks sank in around her teeth. She was nearly flat chested beneath her thin tee shirt. Angel had been too thin, but this poor woman was a stick figure.

The brunette was better off, but not by much. Her long, dark hair had been washed recently, and it still had some luster. Her wide, brown eyes that seemed sad and resigned. Instead of sharing her friend's delight at the loft home, she fell back against the wall and sighed.

"Can you walk?" he asked.

She shrugged.

"It's her knee," the blonde said. "She's not bitten or anything."

Kevin tried to smile. "Let me help you down the stairs." He took her arm and started for the stairway. "Wait." He hadn't slept in the room since Angel had gone. Closing his eyes, he considered the options.

"What's wrong? Is something wrong?"

He shook his head no. "I'm thinking. I'm trying to figure out where to put you. Can you two share a bed?"

The blonde looked at the brunette and laughed. "A bed? Damn!"

Kevin led them to the master bedroom. He opened the door and pointed inside. "It's yours," he said.

The blonde led her friend into the room. He heard them squeal at the sight of a double bed with sheets and blankets. "Holy shit! This is awesome!" At the sound of the shout, Jessica began to cry.

"Oh, I'm sorry," the blonde said. "Did I wake your baby?"

"No. It's just been a long day. Why don't you two get situated? I'm going down to change and feed her."

"What's the baby's name?" the blonde called.

"Jessica."

"Oh my God!" the blonde shouted. "That's my name! What are the odds of that?"

Slim odds these days, Kevin thought.

<hr>

The girls made themselves welcome. The blonde insisted that he call her Jessie *("That way the baby can have her full name!")* while she searched the kitchen, taking stock of her new home. When she came to the pantry, she squealed. "Holy shit! You have food here! What is all of this stuff?"

"Rice, dried beans, a few canned vegetables. Flour. Some granola bars."

"I haven't had a granola bar in a year!" she said, tearing open the wrapper, devouring the bar in two bites. "Do you want one Mindy?"

The brunette gave him a questioning look. He nodded.

Jessie threw her a bar. "That was *so* good. I could eat about a dozen of those."

"I don't think there are more than a few left."

"None left," Jessie said, opening a second wrapper. "Unless you've got more stashed in a spare room. These were the last three. Have you got more food?"

"No. But I know where to get more." He thought of the grocery store he'd just raided. There was plenty of food there. He started to tell them about it, but stopped.

"I'm thirsty as hell," Jessie said, swallowing the second bar as quickly as the first. "What do you have to drink?"

"The cupboard is behind you," he said.

"What?"

"The tap works."

"You're fucking kidding me! You have running water?"

174

"The house has its own well."

The women looked at each other, shaking their heads. "You have quite a setup here," Mindy said. Her voice was small and solemn.

Kevin shrugged. "We don't have a lot of food."

"Trust me. You have plenty." Jessie stood looking into the pantry. "Plenty of beans, for sure."

"Dried beans will last forever. They have some protein in them. I make burritos."

"You have tortillas? I *love* tortillas!"

"I make them."

Jessie shook her head. "Like I said; what a setup."

Mindy sat down near the living room window. The sun was already low in the sky. A white-throated sparrow went sailing past the window, curving out over the water far below.

"Where have you been staying?" he asked. "Before this, I mean."

Mindy started to speak, but Jessie interrupted her. "Around. Here and there."

Mindy looked at her, a question in her eyes.

Kevin shrugged. "I've been here for about six months."

Mindy turned back to the window.

"You haven't boarded anything up in here," Jessie said. "Aren't you afraid they'll get in? The dead, I mean."

"The drop's too steep. The only way around is by the porch on the side of the house. And I walled that up pretty good."

"You have a porch?"

He nodded. The questions were draining him. He'd already spoken more in the last ten minutes than he had in the previous month. Still, not answering would be ungracious. "It's just a small little patio. It has a picnic table, a few chairs and a fire pit."

"A fire pit? Like for barbecue?"

"Yeah," Kevin said. The word barbecue struck him with the force of a hammer blow. He remembered the sweet, smoky flavor of pork ribs. What would he give for a beer and a plate of ribs? A year of his life? The rest of it? He wondered if there were any pigs left on the planet. Surely they were gone, an entire species fallen victim to the

175

plague. Or did the dead eat animals? Who knew?

"You must have been rich before the shit hit the fan." Jessie stood in front of the kitchen counter; her elbows back on the countertop, her small chest thrust forward, her hips cocked to the side.

She's flirting, he realized. *And she's so very out of luck.*

Jessica woke and began to cry. "Wow, that baby of yours cries a lot."

"Actually, she's a very quiet baby," Kevin said, crossing the room to the baby.

"If you say so."

Mindy broke in. "We lived at the stadium."

Kevin stared. "Hughes Stadium?" He turned to Jessie. "Just up the road?"

Jessie looked stricken.

"We've been there for months," Mindy said. Kevin looked into her brown eyes, but couldn't read them.

He turned back to Jessie. "Who's the artist?"

Jessie broke into a sly smile. "The artist?"

"The murals on the side of the stadium."

Jessie laughed. "You like the pictures?"

Kevin held baby Jessica in his arms. He stared into her tiny eyes. *Did I make a mistake, little girl? Who are these people?* Jessica stopped crying at his touch. He sniffed the air once. She needed changing again. He would run out of diapers soon. "I've been trying to figure out what the paintings mean."

"They're about eating," Jessie said. "That's what caused the Apocalypse. Consumption. Some people ate food they didn't need while other people went to bed without eating at all. People ate up the resources of the planet and left their shit everywhere. Even our religions were all about eating. Do you know what Communion is? People go to church and eat the little cookie and drink the grape juice, and it's supposed to be the body and blood of Jesus?"

"That explains the cross." Kevin spoke in a calm, flat voice. He kept his eyes on the baby.

"I painted them," Jessie said. "Most of them, anyway."

"They look like they were painted in blood."

"Clever boy."

Kevin squinted and frowned. "Whose blood?"

"Zombie blood."

Kevin turned back to Mindy. She sat still, her injured knee propped with a pillow. "If you're hungry, I can cook something. Would you like a burrito?"

Mindy nodded.

Kevin went to the kitchen and pulled a pack of rough-shaped tortillas wrapped in saran from the cupboard, working one-handed.

"Do you want me to hold her?" Jessie asked.

Kevin shook his head. "No thanks." He carefully unfolded the plastic wrap, crinkled with use, and pulled out two tortillas. "I don't have any cheese," he said. "But I have beans and a little sauce from a can."

"Are the tortillas home made?" Jessie asked. When Kevin nodded, she added, "Well! Aren't you just the little home maker?"

Kevin looked up, irritation in his eyes. "I didn't make the tortillas. The baby's mother did."

"Where is she?" Mindy asked. A hint of sadness in her voice made it clear that she knew the answer to the question.

"She died giving birth."

"Did she come back?" Jessie asked.

Kevin nodded. He took a scoop of brown flakes from a bulk bin in the pantry and then added them to some tap water in a small saucepan. "I have a little propane hibachi on the balcony. I'll be back in a moment." He took the baby and the pan to the small room under the master bedroom. The former occupants of the home had used the room as an office. The far wall was marred with two bullet holes and smears of brown and black that had soaked into the painted plaster.

The balcony was an eight-by-ten projection that hung out over the steepest part of the incline to the reservoir. He fired up the little grill and set the beans on top. "I couldn't leave them outside," he whispered to Jessica. "This isn't what I wanted. But you can't turn your back when people show up at your door."

Later, Mindy nibbled at her burrito while Jessie shoveled hers in, raving about the food while she chewed. "This is so good! What kind of beans were those? You just added water?"

"Dehydrated refried beans. I don't have a lot, but this seemed like a special occasion."

"Mister, believe me, you have a *lot* of food here. We've been on the edge of starvation *forever*. I thought the zombies were the only ones eating well these days."

"I think they just bite. I don't think they get any substance out of it."

"That's so true," Jessie said. "Just like us, before the Apocalypse. Eating and eating and not getting anything out of it."

Kevin shrugged.

"Is there more food?"

"You ate everything I cooked."

"Aren't you going to eat?"

"I'm on a diet," Kevin said. It was meant as a joke. No one laughed.

"It's going to be dark soon," Mindy said. "Do you have candles?"

"We had them," Kevin said. "They were gone the first week."

"What kind of defenses do you have?" Jessie asked. "Against the zombies, I mean."

"The shamblers stopped coming around a few months ago. Your arrival might stir them up a little, but the door is sturdy and there are no windows on the front of the house. I leave them alone and they eventually wander off."

"Why do you call them shamblers?"

"They shamble." He took Jessica to the big chair in the living room. "I'm going to change her," he warned Mindy. "She pooped."

"Oh hell, that smells gross," Jessie said.

"Do you want some help?" Mindy asked.

"No," Kevin said, regretting the abrupt sound of his voice as soon as he spoke. *I don't know how to talk to people anymore. I wish Angel were here. She'd talk to these women and they'd leave me alone.*

"Where are you going to sleep tonight?" Jessie asked.

"Jessica sleeps on the couch. I sleep on the floor next to her. I think my snoring makes her feel safe."

"Well. You could always join us upstairs." Jessie gave him her sly smile again.

Kevin looked to Mindy. She stared at him, searching his face for a reaction.

"No thank you."

"Suit yourself," Jessie said, clearly miffed. "It doesn't matter to me either way." She glared at Mindy. "Are you coming up?"

"In a few minutes."

"I see. Well then." Without another word, Jessie climbed the stairs, the sway of the hips propelling her forward. She gave them one last glance over the shoulder, tossed her hair and went into the bedroom, closing the door.

"I'm sorry."

Kevin sat down on the floor next to the big stuffed chair. "No reason to apologize. I'm not very good company. I'm out of practice."

"You're in mourning." She turned away, watching as the sun's glow slipped below the mountains to the west.

Jessica nestled in Kevin's arms. Mindy sat without moving. The evening was quiet, nearly peaceful, until a shambler bumped against the front door.

"They do that sometimes," Kevin explained.

"It's creepy. You should build a fence." Her voice came from a darkened silhouette, visibly shaken by the sound.

"Fences don't work."

"You can't just let them in."

"The door is solid. And I have other defenses in place."

"Something good, I hope."

Kevin placed Jessica on the stuffed chair without waking her. Fumbling on the ground, he found her blanket. He rolled it up and wedged it against her so she wouldn't roll off the chair. "Your friend is full of shit about those paintings."

"Why do you say that?"

"Shamblers don't bleed much. And she's no artist."

Silence.

"Why did she lie?"

"She lies about everything. She lies when the truth would serve her." Mindy's voice was soft and melancholy—the sound of a lament.

179

"Her name's not Jessie, by the way. She lied about that, too. Her name is Amber."

"I don't understand."

"Like I said, she lies."

Kevin thought for a moment. "Who's the real artist?"

"His name is Casey."

"How many people live at the stadium?"

"A few. There used to be more. Lots more. People tend to die these days."

"Why did you leave?"

She drew in a breath. It could have been involuntary, the dread of an inevitable question. Or it could have been a sigh, or even a sob. She waited a moment before speaking. "They told me to go. There's no food. Jessie and I are two mouths that can't be fed. They told us that if we returned, we'd better have food."

Kevin considered her answer.

"Do you ever think about what it takes to survive?" she asked.

"Pardon?"

"What does it cost? What does a person have to do to keep living? What do they have to give up? Have you thought about it? I think about it a lot."

He didn't answer.

"Before the zombies came, I was a waitress. There are a lot of rules to being a waitress—things most people don't realize unless they've been in the business. You make your living on tips, but if some jerk stiffs you, you can't say anything. The customer is always right. It's the only commandment on the stone tablet of restaurants. That means the waitress is almost *never* right. You can go to the cooler and scream like a banshee, but you have to smile and apologize if some cretin wants to make your life miserable.

"And there are nuances. Guys can know your name, but they can't touch you. You can't sit with them. You have to be friendly, but you can't be accessible."

"Sounds like tough work." *What does this have to do with the people at the stadium?*

"You know what the Apocalypse was? It was the end of rules. No more laws. No more subtle nuances. If you want to survive, then you have to understand that."

"I've found that you have to make your own laws and stick to them."

"That's the old way." Her voice had taken on a bitter edge. The sun was gone now, and the room was black. "If there are lines you won't cross, you'll die. If you'll do anything, *anything* to survive, you might make it. Or you might not.

"Jessie does what she can to survive. The things that have worked for her are lies and sex. So she sticks with a winning formula.

"She was ready to sleep with you tonight. And she changed her name to match your daughter's name so you'd like her."

"And what works for you? Candor?"

Mindy snorted. "You're funny."

Kevin sat next to the big chair, his head on the cushion. "No, I'm tired."

"Would you mind terribly if I slept on the couch down here?"

"I thought you'd want to try that bed out."

"I'd like a night without Jessie," she said without explaining further.

"I snore."

"Your baby likes it. I might like it, too."

He nodded, and then realized that she couldn't see him. "Will your knee be okay on the couch?"

"My knee is fine."

"There should be a blanket there on the couch."

"There is. Thank you. Good night."

"Goodnight to you," he said. He stretched out on the floor. It was almost chilly in the room. Winter would come in a month or two. He'd need a blanket of his own soon. *How will I keep Jessica warm in the winter? This place doesn't have a fireplace.* He curled up on the floor and let fatigue take him. He had to admit, having Mindy in the room helped. He didn't like sleeping alone.

As he was about to doze off, she asked, "Do you know what a 'wandaco' is?"

"No," he muttered.

She was quiet for a while. Then she said, "It has something to do with Indians. You know. Native Americans?"

He nodded, knowing she couldn't see him. Then he slipped away.

He woke to the sound of someone on the stairs. The room was black. He heard steps going up. The fog wouldn't leave his head. Had Jessie (Amber?) come down? Was she angry at sleeping alone?

He rubbed his eyes. Jessica was silent. Was she all right? He patted the cushion, finding her leg. She stirred at his touch.

The front door creaked.

He stood up, swaying. *What the hell?*

Whispers, loud as a shout in the silence of the house. *Where is the Ruger?* He'd left it on the counter. He crept across the room to the kitchen counter and began patting the stone surface, looking for the gun. He circled the counter, touching everywhere. The Ruger wasn't there. *Where did I leave it?*

His hand closed over the crowbar. Someone had taken the gun. He grabbed the crowbar and headed for the stairs.

Wait. Mindy was asleep on the couch behind him. Should he warn her?

The door closed again. He scowled and crept up the stairs. Step by step, he rose above the living room, trusting the carpeted stairs to keep his ascent a secret. He tried not to breathe. He thought he heard a sound coming from the bedroom. When he reached the top of the stairs, he turned left. Had Amber let someone in?

A flashlight blinded him. He stepped forward, crowbar raised. A sudden blow caught him from behind. His head seemed to explode. He felt himself fall sideways, tumbling back down the stairs. His left arm snapped in the fall. When his head struck the wrought-iron railing, he lost consciousness.

||||||||||||||||||||||||||||||||

"Can you hear me?"

He didn't answer or open his eyes. He tried to lay still. If he moved the arm, he'd grimace or cry out.

The toe of a boot caught him just below the ribs. He twisted away and then cried out from the sharp pain in his arm.

"You can hear me just fine." The man's voice was throaty, as if whittled from a lifetime of cigarettes and whiskey. His sweat smelled like sweet meat. Kevin opened one eye. The man wore the clothing of a professional, fine cotton shirt and pants, topped by a wool vest stitched with Indian symbols. He'd pulled his blonde hair back in a ponytail. The man was filthy, from his forehead to his steel-toed boots. He looked familiar in a way that Kevin couldn't place. *Do I know this man?*

"Hell of a setup you have here, man. Food and shelter? Running water?" He raised his right arm and gave his armpit a sniff. "Hell, I could take a shower here, couldn't I? How about you? Do you shower?"

Kevin didn't answer.

"Yeah, people like you don't smell, do you?"

"You're Casey, I assume?"

The question caught the man off guard, but only for a moment. "That's me." He puffed his chest out. He might have been a body builder before the Apocalypse. His chest and arms hinted at the muscle that once graced the body before hunger and six months of hiding had shriveled him. Only his lips remained fleshy. His puffy, thick-lipped mouth curled into a grin.

"Where's my daughter?" Kevin tried to sit up. The pain in his arm was excruciating. He braced the bad arm with the good one as he rose.

"Stay down," Casey said. "Mindy's got her. She's just fine. But you stay down."

Kevin looked back. Mindy sat on the couch. Jessica lay in her arms, feeding from a bottle. Mindy's face was as blank as the pale sky in the window behind her.

"You didn't need to break in. I invited the women in."

Casey shook his head in disbelief. "Really? A guy living alone lets two women into his little hideaway? What a generous guy you are."

"It's not like that. Ask them."

The blonde stepped out of the bedroom and walked down the stairs, her hips swinging and a smirk on her face. "He's telling the truth, Casey. He could have had us both."

"Is he gay?" Casey seemed to consider the question, but his eyes had a mocking look.

"No, I think he was in love. But his wife is just another zombie now." She stood behind Casey and wrapped her arms around him. She leaned in close and rested her lips on his neck.

"My name is Casey Gardner. Professor Casey Gardner, formerly of Colorado State University. I taught Cultural Studies."

"Did you know Todd Smith?"

"Smith? I knew him. He wasn't tenured."

Kevin nodded.

"But that's the past. The past doesn't matter."

Kevin listened. He kept his eyes on Casey. He had the Ruger tucked in his belt. Maybe the man would shoot himself in the leg.

"I believe you know Amber."

"I must have heard the name wrong."

Casey smirked. "I'm told you're a good cook. Why don't you get up and make me some of these burritos I've been hearing about?"

Kevin stood up. The pain in his arm cut him from elbow to shoulder. He let out a whimper. Amber laughed. Kevin stared at her. *Is she that cruel?* he wondered. *I may be in real trouble.*

Casey tilted his head and tapped the Ruger. "No funny business."

Kevin nodded and headed for the kitchen. *If he lets me get close, I'll hit him with a pan.* Kevin fumbled in the pantry for more dried beans and then fished a pot from under the cupboard. He chose the largest saucepan. He didn't dare look up. If Casey caught him staring, he might guess what was coming. *I'll hit him. Then I'll get the gun.*

As he started around the corner, the front door opened up. Two more men and another woman filed in. One of the men was dressed in camouflage. He carried a rifle. "The area's clear, boss," he called. "There's a construction site just down the road. We found some cool stuff." Kevin stopped, looking up. *Shit. How many are there?*

Casey stared at him, his eyes narrowed. Then he smiled. "You'll have to use that pot for burritos, won't you?"

"Am I feeding them too?"

"Do they look hungry?"

They looked *starved.* The people on the loft gripped the railing, eyes locked on the pot, their clothing hanging in strips from their skeletal bodies.

Kevin returned to the pantry and poured the rest of the beans into the pot. Then he shuffled past Casey, half expecting to be struck from behind.

As he walked to the balcony, he stole a glance at Mindy. Her eyes were on the baby.

When Kevin returned, he spread the rest of his tortillas on the counter and began folding bean burritos. "How many people upstairs?" he asked.

"Five."

Kevin nodded. *I'm fucked.* He cleared his throat. "Clearly, you want the place. All I want is my daughter. Let us go. You can have the place. I'm not territorial. There's running water here. It's defensible. Just let us go."

"I don't think so."

Kevin stopped and turned to face the man. "You have the gun. You have the house. You don't need another two mouths to feed. Let us go. Please."

Amber's hands rested on Casey's chest. She leaned in and bit his earlobe, her gaze on Kevin at every moment. Kevin blinked. Casey *had* looked familiar. He looked enough like Amber to be her brother.

Casey's eyes narrowed again. "I already told you, you're not going anywhere. Now hurry up. My people are hungry."

Kevin nodded. "I have nine burritos. Somebody gets two."

"That would be me," Casey said, his thick lips wet with anticipation. "Set ours right here on the counter. Then take the others upstairs."

Kevin's pushed three of the burritos toward Casey and Jessie. He turned with one for Mindy.

"Leave hers on the counter."

Kevin nodded.

"He likes Mindy," Amber said. "They stayed up all night talking."

"I don't blame him," Casey said. "Mindy's husband liked her, too." Kevin gathered the other burritos on a plate. "You know what happened to her husband?"

"I can imagine," Kevin mumbled.

"Mindy? Tell this guy what happened to your husband."

"He was eaten," Mindy said. Her face betrayed nothing. No fear. No anger.

"So you see, Mindy depends on us for protection." Suddenly, Casey pushed Amber away. Her face flushed with surprise. She kept her hands on him, caressing, leaning back into him and finally clutching him close. When she put her lips back to his neck, she closed her eyes.

"Were you watching closely?" Casey asked. "Did you learn anything?"

Kevin nodded and carried the plate of burritos to the stairs. Amber touched Casey's neck with her tongue. "Why are you so mean?" she asked.

The three people at the loft rail pulled their burritos from the plate before he reached the top step. Kevin started for the door.

"Don't let him outside," Amber called. "He'll run for it."

"No he won't," Mindy said. "He won't leave the baby."

Casey gave Amber another shove. She stepped back, pouting. "Mindy has the baby. He's not going anywhere."

Kevin went to the door and turned, his hand on the wall, next to the burglar alarm. "Why don't you take these?" he asked the man with the rifle. "Maybe someone won't want one, and you'll get two." The two men and the woman hurried out of the door, plate in hand. Kevin shut the door behind them, flipped the lid on the small panel by the front door and pushed all three buttons.

Ray and Peggy Jenkins built their dream home two city blocks down the road, toward the marina. The couple wanted to build green, so they used recycled building materials, put in extra insulation and made plans to install energy efficient appliances and triple-pane windows. Kevin knew this, because their notes to the builders were pinned to the wooden frame in a dozen places around the home, along with snapshots and magazine clippings. The Jenkins family loved the home from its conception to its stillbirth.

The shell of the home stood abandoned after the Apocalypse. Kevin passed it several times before ever venturing inside. It hadn't occurred to him to pick over the construction site for something he could use. The Jenkins' home turned out to be a treasure trove of raw materials. He used cinder blocks and wire to seal off the walkway that led from the porch to the downstairs office window—the only way into the house besides the front door. He used cement rebar to reinforce the window itself.

Kevin kept an informal inventory of the materials in his head. He would never use most of them. But when he searched the dirty white jeep parked near the home's wellhead, he found six blasting caps under the seat. An idea came to him. He thought about the best way to proceed for nearly a week before beginning the project.

First, he pulled conduits from the walls of the home site, burying them in trenches he'd dug in his lawn. He used receptical boxes to hold the charges. He fashioned the control panel from a neighbor's burglar alarm.

The blasting powder was more difficult. He found what he needed on Overland. A Legacy on the south side of the stadium had reloading equipment for firearms packed in the trunk, along with three cans of black powder. Kevin loaded the receptical boxes with assorted bullets, as well as some old-fashioned fishing line weights taken from a tackle box. He waterproofed his contraption with plastic tarp.

Kevin placed two of the makeshift mines in a crossfire pattern in the shrubs to either side of the door. He placed the third charge at one edge of the driveway, pointed back towards the house. Some of the pellets would clear the edge of the roof. Chances were good that if he ever needed to trigger the system, it would be used against a crowd of shamblers. But if human marauders were involved, strafing the flat of the roof would be a good thing.

‖‖‖‖‖‖‖‖‖‖‖‖‖‖‖‖‖‖‖‖

The detonations rocked the house. Lead pellets sounded against the stone like a volley. The sound shocked Kevin as much as the others. He'd never tested the panel—he didn't have enough powder. Casey and Jessie stood at the bottom of the stairs, mouths open. Casey hadn't drawn the Ruger.

Kevin flung himself down the stairs, two at a time, crying out from the pain as his broken arm waved helplessly. He slammed into Casey, knocking him back into the living room.

"What's happening?" Amber screamed.

Casey sat up, fumbling for the pistol. Kevin scuttled across the floor, lashing out with his foot. Casey caught it, grunting, throwing Kevin back. Panicked, Kevin threw himself on Casey again, pummeling him with his one good fist.

Casey grabbed the bad arm and squeezed.

Kevin screamed, twisting away. The white-hot flash of pain blinded him. He couldn't breathe. *Get up! Get up!* He managed to get the good arm under him and push up. He was on his knees when the boot struck him in the temple.

॥॥॥॥॥॥॥॥॥॥॥॥॥॥॥॥॥॥

"You should never have let the women in," Casey said.

Kevin's eyes fluttered. He started to move but it was too painful. He put a hand to his head. It came away sticky.

"Can you stand?"

They were outside. Someone had carried him out. Kevin could feel the soft breath of a fall evening on his skin. His arm still ached, but he was half asleep. The pain would come on soon enough.

"Get up."

"I'll try," Kevin said. He rolled to the side and groaned. His hip ached. His arm screamed. And his head felt as if it had been stuffed with razors. He took a deep breath and stood, trying not to vomit. They'd gathered at the side of the house, near the patio. Casey and Amber faced him, arm in arm. Mindy stood off to the side, baby Jessica in her arms. Two survivors of the blast stood, rifles pointed. Further down the driveway, three bodies were stacked together. One of the corpses was the man in camouflage.

Casey followed his gaze. "You got three out of five. Pretty good. They won't reanimate either. Their heads were blasted all to shit."

Kevin tried to stand straight. The breeze threatened to pitch him back down on the ground.

"You're going to pay for what you did," Amber said. She had a leering grin that turned her thin, emaciated face into a skull.

"You don't have to starve, you know." Kevin's voice was a papery whisper.

"I know. We could be rich and live in a nice house."

"It wasn't my house. I moved in when the owners didn't need it anymore."

"Amber tells me that you knew we were living in the stadium. She says you looked at my paintings."

Kevin took a ragged breath and tried again. "There's plenty of food in town. More than I could carry."

"Yeah. And anyone who goes after it becomes food for the zombies."

"No. The zombies are dying. Again. They're dying again." The odd thought seized him, and his cracked lips ached with a half smile.

"You just don't get it, do you? Our time is over. It's *their* time. If you want to live, you have to give up the past."

"I can do that," Kevin promised.

"I'm not talking about you, fuck head. I'm talking about *my* people."

Kevin glanced at the baby. *I hope they take care of her when I'm gone.* Then he thought, *She won't know me. She'll be one of them.*

"We had to change. We had to do things we didn't think we could do. That's how you survive." He looked around to make sure the others were listening. "People like you brought the Apocalypse on. Greedy, rich fucks like you. Now, three of us are dead. Again, because of greedy, rich fucks like you."

"I opened up this house to your people," Kevin said, a hitch in his voice. He felt as if he might burst into tears.

"It's a new world, you son of a bitch. We take what we need. We live like the dead. It's *their* world now. As for you, your time is over. You and the dinosaurs."

"I tried to do the right thing."

"*I tried to do the right thing,*" Casey mimicked in a whiney voice. Amber smirked. "It's the time of the Wendigo. Do you know the Wendigo?" He rushed on, without waiting for an answer. "The Wendigo is a Native American spirit that can possess humans and make them eat flesh. And those who eat flesh are more succeptible to possession. Do you understand? The Apocalypse is the red man's revenge. The white man ate the planet alive. Now the planet is eating him right back."

Oh, God! It's just another theory—one more fucked up theory to explain what can't be explained.

"Nothing to say?"

"You look pretty Aryan to me." Kevin felt weak. He started to drop back down, knees bent. The ground looked soft.

"Stand up!" Casey ordered. His face shook with anger. Kevin stood tall, on demand.

"Turn around."

Kevin turned. Someone had put a corrugated tub on the patio. He recognized it from the construction site. Workers had used it to stock sodas. Kevin had found an old Mountain Dew inside. He gave it to Angel as a present.

"Now look at me."

Kevin turned back.

"This is the age of the Wendigo. The walking dead are his children."

Kevin shrugged.

"We have new rules," he said, playing to the others.

Pathetic, Kevin thought. *A messiah with four followers.* The sun hung on the rim of the mountains. The breeze chilled him. A mosquito buzzed his ear. "You don't need to starve. There's food in town."

"Yes there is. Take Mindy's husband." He turned back, grinning. "How did he taste, my dear?"

"Like chicken." Her face was as blank as Kevin's future.

Casey burst out laughing. "She always says that. And it's always funny. Do you understand? Now walk back there to the porch. Go on."

Kevin stumbled back to the porch. The galvanized tub had been placed over the fire pit. The tub was full of water. A fire had the water at a boil.

"Take off your clothes."

Kevin turned back, his face burning. "Fuck you."

"Don't forget your baby," Casey said. "Do it."

Kevin looked at Mindy. She gave him no sign of hope. He fumbled with the buckle of his jeans, one-handing the button and zipper.

"Yeah, that's the way." Amber seemed pleased with his

embarrassment.

He pulled off his pants and shirt. The shirt came off slowly, each wincing move a blow to his broken arm.

"The underwear, too."

Kevin slipped the shorts off. His genitals shrank in the cold. He covered himself with his hands, shivering. Amber stifled a laugh, covering her mouth with both hands.

"Mindy, how is the baby?"

Kevin started forward, but Casey held up one hand and pointed at the baby with the other. "Kirkus?"

One of the men leveled his rifle.

"If he moves toward me again, shoot the baby." Casey put his hands behind his back. "We eat people. Does that shock you?"

"There are groceries in town. I could get food and bring it to you. You could keep the baby to guarantee my return. You don't have to do this."

"At first, we didn't want to eat like that. But we ran out of canned goods."

"There's plenty of food!"

"It's a new age. We eat the way we are meant to eat."

"It's wrong. What you're doing is wrong."

"There is no right or wrong. There's dead and alive. And the dead eat very well."

"Why are you doing this?"

"You killed my people. And the ones you didn't kill are hungry. This was all predicted. I am the last of the prophets. I remember what was said and I know what will be." He rubbed his hands together. "Now get in the tub."

"Shoot me," Kevin said.

"I don't think so." Casey pointed at Jessica once more. "Climb in the tub and cook, and we'll take care of your daughter. You have my word. We'll look after her and raise her as our own. But if I have to shoot you, I'll cook your daughter."

"There are three dead bodies over there on the driveway, if you're so damned hungry for flesh!"

Casey's eyes narrowed. "They're *family*. Now climb in the tub."

"You can't do this." Kevin's face went slack with horror.

"I mean it. And you have five seconds to decide."

Kevin stood staring at the tub. The fire pit roared beneath the steel. The water in the tub had come to a rolling boil. Steam rose off the vat into the cool night air. "My daughter will live?"

"If you stay in the tub. If you get back out, we'll cook her."

Kevin looked at Casey. "People don't do this to each other."

"They do it all the time."

Kevin took a deep breath and stuck one leg in, then pulled it out as quickly as he could. The skin was pink and steaming. He groaned, tears leaking from his eyes.

"That's it," Casey said, turning to the baby.

"No!" Kevin shouted. He steeled himself and then climbed into the boiling water. His screams rose as he lowered himself into the vat. Once, twice he seemed poised to pitch back out, but his good arm locked him in place, shaking with the effort. He called out to God in a single, piercing scream. Steam obscured his face, but the cost of his struggle was evident in the way his fingers locked onto the side of the vat while his broken arm flopped helplessly in the boiling water.

Amber turned away. Mindy watched.

"Damn!" Casey said. "I didn't think he'd do it. I really didn't. I mean, what the fuck! *Look at that!*"

The man in the boiling vat slipped down into the water, leaving half of his face beneath the surface.

"Very well done," Casey said, approaching the vat. "He really must love his daughter."

Kevin convulsed in the water.

"What about the baby?" Amber asked.

Casey put his hands on his hips. "Let her join her father," he said.

Mindy paused. Her eyes betrayed a moment of pure horror. She looked at the baby once, as if the sight had the power to destroy her. Her face went slack. Her mouth opened and her head hung down. She stumbled forward, trembling steps to the boiling vat, unwrapping the bundled infant.

And she did as she was told.

ACKNOWLEDGEMENTS

I need to thank a few people. The Raintree Writers is an amazing critique group comprised of five women who would not normally read a zombie novel. Yet they did so with great cheerfulness and enthusiasm. Pat Stoltey, Carolyn Yalin, Melissa Pattison, Bev Marquart and April Joitel were good and patient readers.

My other critique group, the Penpointers, was equally helpful. Jason Richter, Ross Willard and Aaron Spriggs gave me food for thought from start to finish.

A special thanks is in order for two other people. Nancy Crenshaw is a fine writer/editor who did a cover-to-cover reading for me. And Ken Harmon did a line-by-line edit. Without their efforts, the book would have been less than it is.

Thanks also to Corey Graham of the Midnight Podcast. Google his name and start listening to his weekly show. Corey is an exuberant fan of the zombie apocalypse (and the Pittsburg Steelers). Whenever my energy flagged, Corey stoked the fires.

Thanks to George Romero for ruining several nights sleep every month for the last forty years. I hope this book "pays it forward" for some young, impressionable reader.

Thanks to Charles Kaine of Last Knight Publishing for helping me get this book off the ground, and to Michael St. Clair for the nifty book design.

Finally, thanks to Jack Larson for the sick cover art. You rock.

ALSO BY
BRIAN KAUFMAN

The Breach (2002)

The Apocalypse Parable (2006)

Marketing Principles (2008)

ABOUT THE AUTHOR

Brian Kaufman lives with his
wife and dog in the mountains
of Colorado. He makes his living
as a curriculum editor for a
distance learning college. As a
freelance writer, he has published
in numerous newspapers and
magazines. His first novel, *The
Breach* (Last Knight Publishing,
2002), tells the story of the Alamo
from the Mexican point of view.
His second novel, *The Apocalypse
Parable* (Last Knight Publishing,
2006), follows a low-rent private
investigator's search for the

Second Coming of Jesus. Brian also authored a textbook, *Marketing
Principles* (Weston Distance Learning, 2007).

You can find Brian on his Facebook page (Brian Kaufman), or at
Last Knight Publishing (http://www.lastknightpublishing.com) or
at Dark Silo Press (http://www.darksilopress.com).